GLADIATOR ISLAND

The Triangle

COREY O'NEILL

EPIC
Press

The Triangle
Gladiator Island: Book #4

Written by Corey O'Neill

Published by EPIC Press™
PO Box 398166
Minneapolis, MN 55439

Printed in the United States of America.

Cover design by Laura Mitchell
Images for cover art obtained from iStockPhoto.com
Edited by Leah Jenness

Library of Congress Cataloging-in-Publication Data

Names: O'Neill, Corey, author.
Title: The triangle / by Corey O'Neill.
Description: Minneapolis, MN : EPIC Press, [2017] | Series: Gladiator Island ; book #4
Summary: One of Reed's closest allies has a secret, and it could destroy any chance Reed and
   his friends have of ever escaping the island. This person hasn't been what they've seemed
   since the very beginning, and will do anything they can to stop Reed and the others from
   leaving.
Identifiers: LCCN 2015959400 | ISBN 9781680762709 (lib. bdg.) |
   ISBN 9781680762914 (ebook)
Subjects: LCSH: Adventure and adventurers—Fiction. | Interpersonal relationships—Fiction. |
   Survival—Fiction. | Human behavior—Fiction. | Young adult fiction.
Classification: DDC [Fic]—dc23
LC record available at http://lccn.loc.gov/2015959400

EPIC
Press

For Liberty

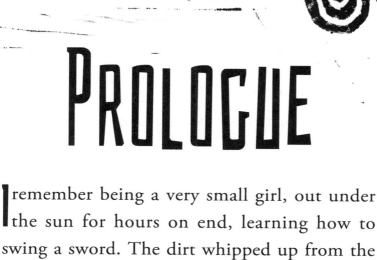

PROLOGUE

I remember being a very small girl, out under the sun for hours on end, learning how to swing a sword. The dirt whipped up from the ground when it was windy, stinging my eyes and covering my skin.

When I wanted to quit, Titus and True convinced me to keep on going. I pushed through the pain to please them.

Those were among my first recollections of what life was like in the Triangle.

Our days were repetitive—just like this.

Titus and True woke us up before the Littles. We got dressed in gray cotton shorts and t-shirts, and ate a filling breakfast—eggs, oatmeal, and whatever fruit was growing in the small greenhouse perched at the very tip of the island. It overlooked the sea, next to the small bunker where we lived.

After breakfast, we warmed up as Titus and True took our vital signs—temperature, blood pressure, and the like—and asked us questions about what we were thinking, how we were feeling, if anything hurt, if we had any impulses that needed to be discussed and addressed.

The same inquiries every single day. They typed notes, recorded things in their wristlets, and examined our skin, our muscle tone, and our overall disposition.

After our daily exam, we'd head to the training yard and they'd put us through one physical test after another. Swordplay. Wrestling. Martial arts. Mind games to see how we'd respond and if we'd turn on each other. Micah and I never did.

No matter what they did to try to break the

bond between us, we always, always stuck together and stood up for each other.

I loved him.

After our daily training, we'd sit down for lunch and recount what we did well and what needed to be improved. Micah and I compared mental notes and joked with each other as we stuffed food into our mouths, starving. The meal was reliably simple but hearty. We needed the calories and emptied our plates of every last morsel.

In the afternoons we had "school," as Titus and True called it. We watched videos that taught us how to read and write, that taught us about science and history and mathematics. We also watched movies—so many movies. Probably one or two of them a day. We mimicked the lines, practicing how to say things like normal kids. We did it because we were bored and because teenagers in movies were cooler than us and did interesting things we wished we could do.

After "school," we got to explore the Triangle.

There wasn't much to see, though. There was the building where we lived; it was plain and had rooms for the younger kids and us. There were Titus and True's living quarters, but they didn't stay there all the time. Sometimes they were on the other side, helping Gareth with assignments, all of which were very important, as True liked to remind us.

When Titus was feeling generous, he'd sneak over desserts from the dining hall on the Praeclarus side, and pass them to us when True wasn't around.

True was always grumpy; this was pretty much the rule. He reminded us that he was here to make sure we grew up correctly and to follow Gareth's orders, not to be our friends.

Micah and I poked fun at him behind his back. Titus caught us once and he was livid, berating us for being disrespectful. Titus alternated beating Micah and me, striking our backsides with a cane again and again and again, the skin ripping open and bleeding. I tried not to cry, even though it was fiercely painful. Titus made us repeat again and again: "True is on our side, True is on our side . . ."

CHAPTER 1

Delphine – Age 15

When we arrived in the middle of the night, the air was much colder than I liked. As we prepared to leave the ship for the first time in weeks, I pulled on a hoodie, as teenagers in movies called it. It was a silly name to me.

"Hoodie. Huuuuh-dee. That's an odd word, isn't it?" I asked as I offered up my hand to Micah. He guided me off the boat's ledge and onto the dock.

Solid land. My legs were wobbly, yet it felt nice, and I smiled up at him. He pulled me in for a long hug and then bent down for a kiss.

It never got old kissing him, and I stood up on my toes to meet him halfway.

"Ahem! We don't have time for that right now."

We stopped and turned to Titus, whose arms were folded tightly across his chest, and he looked at us with that pinched, cross expression that we had seen a million times. True stood right behind him, like a tall, angular statue with a permanent scowl etched in his face.

"No time to waste. We have much to do," Titus said as we followed him down the dock to a parking lot, which was dotted with about twenty cars, all empty and dark.

I squeezed Micah's hand. He looked at me and grinned, but put his other finger up to his lips to warn me to play it cool. Titus and True didn't suffer us joking around more than just a little bit. But we were teenagers, and it was inevitable. We had to remind them of that sometimes.

Titus pulled keys out of his pocket and the car beeped, unlocking the doors. I looked around, but there was no one else in sight and the night was quiet and still.

He sat in the driver's seat, True folded his long limbs into the passenger side, and we got in the back. As we drove away, I found the button to put down the window just a little bit and I turned my face up to the cool air, looking out at the black scenery dotted with lights and billboards selling things I'd never seen before. I couldn't help but feel gleeful.

Finally, things were really happening. We were people in action, helping Gareth enact a plan. For years now, I'd begged Gareth to let us leave the Triangle—to put us to work.

And here we were in the middle of the night, in Oregon, somewhere that looked like places I'd seen in movies, but never in real life. I leaned my head on Micah's shoulder, overwhelmed with the feeling of his warm body against mine, and how it still made my heart flutter, like I was completely and undeniably human.

Pretty soon we'd have to pretend like we didn't know each other at all. I was dreading it, but I knew it was what had to be done.

I walked up to the front door of a large, white house with big windows. The lights were on in every downstairs room so I could clearly see kids hanging out, laughing and drinking out of red plastic cups. They were packed in tight, pushing up against each other in a way that felt vulgar. They all looked extremely sweaty and I swear I could smell them, even from my vantage point outside.

It was the most teenagers I'd ever seen and I watched them for a moment, taking it all in. I couldn't delay too much—our plan was depending on me getting this key step right. I heard loud music coming through the walls, and I stood there for a second longer, gearing myself up for what I needed to do.

I looked back toward the end of the driveway, and the black car flashed its headlights at me twice, then it went dark. I was on my own.

I glanced down at my chest and pushed up my boobs so they were practically popping out of the tank top. Micah, Titus, and True had helped me pick out the outfit and reminded me, it was just like the movies. I should look a certain way to be sure I'd get Reed's attention. The blonde wig was ridiculous and as soon as I put it on, I collapsed in a fit of laughter on the couch. But Micah assured me I looked hot, and he was the one that liked girls, so I trusted his judgment.

Here goes nothing, I thought, breathing deeply. It was all so exotic.

I opened the door and walked into the entrance-way like I belonged there. Two girls leaning against a closet door turned to look at me, and I saw their eyes go from my face to my boobs to my tan, bare legs and up again. Their noses pinched in a scowl, but I just smiled at them widely and said "hello."

The smaller girl on the left muttered "hi" back, and I could tell they were puzzled when I walked right past them toward where the music was blaring. I could hear kids screaming conversations over the thick, persistent beats.

"Who is that?" the small girl asked before her voice was engulfed by the thump, thump, thump of the music. It was so loud that it was practically disorienting. It reminded me of one of our audio torture sessions.

Guys and girls were everywhere—chugging down drinks, just like I'd seen a million times in dumb teen movies. They were taking pictures of themselves with their wristlets, making out with each other and stumbling over me. One scrawny kid walking past tripped and wet my leg with his beer.

"Whoa! Sorry little lady!" he said, looking me over like I was something he wanted. "You are smoking hot!" he exclaimed, and leaned his arm against the wall to steady himself. I rolled my eyes and moved on.

Micah and I had watched so many movies about teenagers when we were growing up. This party scene was like those films come to life, and I wished that he could be here with me so we could laugh about how crazy this was.

I felt many sets of eyes on me as I walked across the room to the keg, where I fumbled for a moment to pour myself a beer. *I need to look like I belong here*, I reminded myself as I took a sip from the plastic cup and tried not to grimace.

It was disgusting. I couldn't believe people actually wanted to drink this stuff. I tried to seem cool as I took another bigger gulp and scanned the room, looking for Reed. I'd studied him in pictures and videos, but couldn't find him anywhere. The scruffy brown hair, the long Roman nose and friendly eyes. Where was he? Where was he? Where was he?

"Are you looking for someone?" a boy's voice

asked, hot in my ear, and I started, surprised someone was so close to me. I couldn't hear him approach over the music. I spun around and jumped back. I couldn't believe my luck. It was Reed.

Right there. In the flesh. He put his arm around me and leaned against me. He was wasted. I could smell it on his breath and see it in how he gazed upon me hungrily and sleepily at once.

Well, that makes things easier, doesn't it, I thought to myself as I smiled as sweet as I could muster and pushed my chest out as insurance to ensure his attention wouldn't wander.

"Now, why haven't I seen you before?" Reed asked me. I laughed like a dumb girl who liked to act dumb, and smiled sweetly.

"I don't know, but I'm certain I've never seen you before either. There's no way I could forget you," I said and looked up at him with my cute face, as Micah called it. It was the face I gave Micah when I wanted something badly.

Reed was better looking in person than I expected him to be, and even though he was drunk, I knew that luring him away using the potential for sex as bait was going to be more fun than I anticipated. He was cute, thank goodness.

We flirted for a while and I asked him if he wanted to go outside. He looked at me eagerly. "Of course, but let me get uh nuther drink . . . " He was starting to slur a bit, and stumbled to the keg.

He sloshed another drink into the cup, and we walked out the front door.

"Sweetie, may I have a sip?" I asked.

"Sure thing, uh . . . what's yer name again?" he asked.

"Angel," I said. It was so ridiculous that I laughed to myself. Reed laughed too, but I am pretty certain he didn't know why. When he handed me the drink, I quickly poured in the powder from the vial I'd hidden in my bra and gave it back to him. Not that he'd notice, but I snuck a glance at the cup, and everything had dissolved instantaneously.

This was it, I thought. He took down the disgusting drink in one sip, like he was showing off, and I pretended to be impressed.

"Wow . . . that's really something," I said, and without a second thought, I grabbed onto him and kissed him hard, pushing him up against the garage door. I could feel that his body was muscular and firm under his threadbare t-shirt.

"Woah . . . " he said, and took a step back, smiling. "I like that . . . "

"I know you do, baby," I purred back just like I'd memorized from those cheesy movies, and kissed him more. He stuck his tongue in my mouth and it felt weird having someone other than Micah's lips on mine.

After we made out for a while and I was certain the drugs were taking effect, I took a step back and smiled at him, raising my eyebrows and grinning at him.

"Want to go back to my place?" Reed asked. "It's not . . . far . . . " he mumbled. He seemed like he wanted to say more, but was having trouble getting the words out.

"Sure," I replied. We started to walk down the dark street, but he was stumbling and couldn't get far—just about half a block away from the party house. We had to move quicker.

"I need help," I said into my wristlet, and a minute later, the black car pulled up next to me, its headlights out. Micah swung open the door, and he and True jumped out, grabbing onto Reed. I slid into the front seat and watched them out the window.

Reed was full-on passing out now and didn't resist as the guys slammed him against the car. I sat quietly as they beat Reed—punching him in the face, the stomach, and then the chest again and again. They were doing enough damage to make him look like he'd taken the rough end of a drunken fight, but not enough to send him to the hospital—the abuse was carefully calibrated. We had gone over the plan many times on the island with Gareth.

When they were done, Micah opened the back door and they lifted Reed up and shoved him into the corner of the back seat, and smashed themselves in next to him.

"I think that will do it," Titus said.

It was very late as we pulled up to the driveway of the Mackenzie estate. Tim Mackenzie was a "man of the people," Gareth had explained. He wasn't the type to have a gated entrance. Gareth was right.

The lights in the house were off and we parked far enough away to not trigger the motion sensor floodlights we'd scoped out the night prior.

Micah and True quietly opened the car door, put on ski masks and then pulled a limp Reed out of the car. They took off his clothes and I couldn't help but sneak a look. I turned my head away, embarrassed, when Micah caught my gaze. He rolled his eyes.

"We'll be back in two minutes," True hissed. Titus and I waited in the car in silence as they dragged Reed to the Mackenzie backyard, where his parents were certain to find him the next morning.

I almost felt bad for the guy. He seemed nice enough, but what was done was done. It was ordained by Gareth and Praeclarus. Gareth wanted him on the island, and so that's the way it would be.

This was a unique situation—going out to get Reed to bring him back. Before we left, Gareth reminded us that Tim Mackenzie had had it coming for many, many years, and that Gareth was going to finally right a wrong from both of their pasts. He didn't go into more detail no matter how much we pried, but I didn't care all that much about the reason. I trusted Gareth and I was made to obey.

When Micah asked Titus about Gareth's beef with Tim, he explained that yes, they had some long-standing issue from more than twenty years ago, and Gareth still harbored a deep, bitter resentment. The funniest part about it was that as far as Tim knew, Gareth died in a plane crash years and years ago and their feud died with that plane plunging into the ocean.

But I knew Gareth stealing Reed away wasn't just about Tim.

It was about Praeclarus too.

Titus told us that Gareth was getting paranoid that someone was going to turn on him and would expose the island to the world, so the great lengths he went to in punishing Tim Mackenzie were also a way to warn everyone. Gareth was always thinking, always reminding others of the limitless nature of his power—a message that if you fuck with Gareth, he'll go after your family, and he may just wait and take action when you think all is normal and okay. It may happen tomorrow, or two years from now, or ten, or even thirty years later . . . it would be impossible to predict or protect against forever.

And Micah and I were here to enforce his will.

Instead of fearing Gareth, his awesome power made me love and respect him even more. I mean, he made me. Literally. He was my creator and I was hopelessly devoted to him.

CHAPTER 2

Delphine – Present Day

Sitting here in the Coliseum watching the battles, it was clear to me that Reed was going to lose the fight against the Komodo tiger. Given that I'd been in combat training every day since I was a young child, it was unpleasant watching such a one-sided battle—and one in which Reed, a formerly talented fighter, was rendered practically useless. He was like the animal's rag doll that he played with before finishing him off.

It was plain to see he was about to be torn in pieces. Everyone in the stadium was cheering like crazy as the animal bit down into Reed's leg and shook him hard, causing him to slam to the ground.

I sat there next to Gareth, playing my part like his unwilling lover. My true nature and relationship to him wasn't known by Praeclarus yet, although Gareth promised our big reveal would be coming soon—the grand finale, as he liked to say. For now, I had to keep my real self concealed.

As we watched the fight, I wanted to turn to Gareth and say what I was really thinking—that he was making a huge mistake letting Reed die. The revolt supposedly hinged on getting help from Reed's dad. No matter what I said to Gareth in our private conversations, though, he viewed Reed as a pest that needed to be exterminated immediately.

The truth to me was starkly different. We needed to learn more about what was being planned—and the players involved—in order to punish everyone fully. At this point, we didn't even know how many of the Suits had turned, ready to

kill us if needed. And we didn't know who would still protect us.

Reed talked to me openly—he had no idea. I knew I could help put a stop to the revolt if Gareth would just give it more time and let me work Reed a little longer.

Before the fight, I tried to sway Gareth one last time, but his mind was made up.

I'd never outwardly questioned Gareth's decisions before—ever—but as I saw Reed being dragged across the Coliseum by the scaled and furry creature, I knew without a doubt it was a mistake letting him die. That couldn't happen yet.

Before Gareth understood what was happening and could try to stop me, I jumped down over the wall onto the Coliseum floor, landing with a hard thud. I'd been raised for this—for battle—and I didn't feel any fear, as I knew what I had to do.

"Stop her! But bring her to me alive!" I heard Gareth yell from above, but it was too late. I was faster and more lethal than any Suit, and I got up from the ground and sprinted toward the Komodo tiger, whose giant mouth was clamped onto Reed's shoulder, shaking it violently.

I saw the dagger lying on the ground and snatched it up. The creature was beautiful in action, and I felt a second of remorse for what needed to be done. Was the strange hybrid animal *that* different from me?

I screamed out as I plunged the knife into the animal's neck. It let out the most guttural, terrible scream and I heard people in the crowd gasp. I stabbed it again, this time in the fleshy area of its back, and the animal howled in agony and thrashed its body around to face me.

Just then, Reed grabbed the creature's tail and yanked it, which made the animal turn, confused, as it was now being attacked from two sides. Recognizing my moment to finish the job, I ran forward and sliced the animal's neck cleanly and then plunged the blade into it one last time. Blood spurted from its mouth, its body slowed, and I knew from experience that that was the death blow.

I let go of the weapon and turned toward Reed, who had collapsed just feet away. I ran over and sat next to him, and gingerly lifted his bloody body into my arms. He looked up at me—I could see he was in incredible pain, but he still seemed happy to see me, his lips turning up into a smile just a tiny bit.

"Help him!" I called up to the stands. I saw Gareth scowling at me. I'd explain everything later, I decided, not worried about him. I knew I had done the right thing, keeping Reed alive.

I took no pleasure in killing the creature, and as I sat there on the Coliseum floor, drenched in the blood of Reed and the animal, I did my best to look steely-eyed and resolute. It was what the Praeclarus members liked about me. I was tough. And some of them found that irresistible.

The crowd's cheers were deafening, their

approval clear. I heard them chanting my name again and again.

Suits carrying a stretcher suddenly appeared next to me, and snatched Reed out of from my embrace, roughly pushing me aside.

Remembering this was a performance and the Praeclarus members thought I was Reed's friend— not just keeping him alive for strategy—I suddenly broke and began to cry. I wanted to make sure Reed heard me as he was taken away. He must keep thinking that I'm on his side, and that I had risked my own life to save him. The plan depended on his blind trust in me, a pretty girl that he really didn't know at all.

"Reed . . . oh God . . . please help him!" I yelled, sobbing and screaming out again and again. I cried as loud as I could muster, and the arena grew quiet, all eyes on me. I saw my face projected in extreme close-up on the gigantic screen overhead.

Suddenly, out of the corner of my eye, I spotted

someone in a flowing dress fall to the ground, below the section where Gareth was sitting.

Chelsea. What was she doing?

She started to run toward me, screaming, "This must stop! My dad is a criminal! And so are all of you!"

I stopped crying abruptly and got up halfway, preparing to defend myself. It would be an easy battle since this silly girl had never fought a day in her life. It was a death wish charging me and screaming out against Gareth so publicly, embarrassing him no doubt.

But as she reached me, she didn't attack me but instead wrapped her arms around me in a hug. It felt like she was holding on for dear life, like I was a life preserver and she was going under.

"What are you doing?" I spat at her, and the crowd came to life again. They were certainly getting their money's worth. The shows were more and more dramatic—some of it by Gareth's design, but today, not so much. The chaos was created by me, and then there was Chelsea—out of the blue—making things *really* interesting.

Chelsea pulled my head close to hers and whispered in my ear: "Let's get out of here."

Aha, I thought, satisfied. *I knew it.*

Before I had time to respond, Suits grabbed Chelsea and dragged her away. She was screaming. *Stupid girl*, I thought.

"You've made a huge mistake!" I yelled out at her as they pulled her through the gate.

I had jumped into the Coliseum to ultimately protect Gareth, whereas Chelsea just confirmed to me what I had suspected—she had turned on him. His own biological daughter. I couldn't help but smirk.

I needed to talk about everything with Gareth—to explain my spur-of-the-moment decision to him. But first, I'd go shower and get cleaned up. He hated the smell of blood.

CHAPTER 3

Delphine – Age 14

"But, why can't we see the Praeclarus side of the island again? And what about Chelsea . . . Why is *she* over there and not us?" I asked Gareth, who was busy examining Micah's triceps closely, his face just inches away from it. He pinched the skin and then released it, watching to see how quickly it returned to its normal color. It was one of the many tests done on us every day.

I asked a version of this question every time Gareth came by. Micah rolled his eyes because the answer was always the same set of excuses.

"Delphine, Delphine, Delphine . . . why do you do this to me again and again?" Gareth asked.

"You know why!" I whined.

"You're not here to be entertained, love. If you're bored, you and Micah can use your imaginations. Remember what I say about imagination?"

I was silent, feeling frustrated.

"Delphine?"

"That the world is as big as my mind."

"Exactly," Gareth said, patting me on top of the head.

"Hmph," I said, and sat down under the tree, which shaded us from the midday sun. I was used to the sun, so it didn't bother me all that much, but Gareth liked to protect his skin. He fanned his straw hat in front of his face and looked at me, dismayed.

"Why are you giving me a hard time all of a sudden? I never thought teenage girls could really be the source of so much heartburn. Are you trying

to put me in my grave early?" he joked, and raised his eyebrows at me.

"No! Of course not. That's a terrible thing to say!" I was horrified at the notion. Gareth was the closest thing I had to a dad, and was my lifeline in every way imaginable. Without him, I wouldn't exist. And I'd have nowhere to go. I suddenly felt badly for nagging him again.

"I'm sorry, Gareth." I looked up at him, and he smiled down at me. All was forgiven. That was how we communicated lately. I gave him a hard time, felt guilty about it, and then we made up.

"It's okay, love. But why can't you be more like Micah?" Gareth joked, looking over at Micah, who was stretching out, his tan skin caked with dirt from the morning's training.

Micah smiled goofily and nodded, nudging me in the arm. "Yeah, Delphine?"

He was just toying with me, playing along with Gareth. Micah wanted to see the other side of the island too. We talked about it all the time, but he never asked Gareth himself and instead let me pester on his behalf. I was bad cop and Micah was always good cop.

Ever since I could remember, Titus told us stories of what happened on the other side of the hangar. True always shook his head in disapproval, and sighed heavily whenever we'd ask for more details. We weren't supposed to know about the Praeclarus side of the island at all, but Titus couldn't help himself. He'd wink at us, which would only make True get more worked up. His face would turn beet red, and we'd laugh with Titus. He was one of our only sources of conversation—aside from each other and the random appearances by Gareth.

The wide cement hangar building blocked us from even glimpsing all of the amazing things that spread out across the island on the other side. From over here, in the Triangle, as it was dubbed due to its small, pointy shape—the butt of the island, as Titus joked—all we could see were the tips of green mountains in the distance, peeking over the impossibly tall walls of the hangar, where the scientists lived with the Creatures and the Littles.

Titus shared stories about the men and women from all over the world who came to the other side of the island for their weird "vacations," as he put it. He also told us about people who lived permanently on the other side, always dressed in white suits, and who treated the visitors like royalty. Over dinners, he'd tell us stories of all the buildings and rooms bedazzled in jewels and draped in rich, colorful fabrics. There were giant, beautiful structures over there that supposedly glittered like gold in the evening. And most intriguing to me, Titus recounted stories about how Gareth created a replica of the Roman Coliseum, like in the movies we watched all the time. *Gladiator. Spartacus.* He never said why Gareth built it, though, which drove me crazy.

It all sounded so spectacular to me, so it was torturous having just a large, ugly building and barbed wire fencing separating us from exploring such an enchanting place—a place that Gareth created to please and entertain his friends. I wanted nothing more than to experience it all firsthand.

In the Triangle, life was simple and dull, for the most part. Micah and I were created here, born in a lab in the hangar; it was the only home we'd ever known. My first memories were toddling around the scientists, and being trouser-level, looking up at them as they examined me, running me through tests. It was later explained that I was a miracle. For some reason, Micah and I lived on when others had died. We were the first to survive.

Today, as Gareth sat next to us in the shade of the tree while we took a break from morning training, he was quieter than usual.

The three of us watched the younger kids

fighting each other, wrestling on the ground in pairs.

"They're looking good, Gareth," Micah said, smiling. "It never ceases to amaze, right?"

"No, it does not," Gareth agreed, perking up. He liked nothing more than talking about his creations, and we were his crown jewels.

The field was filled with twenty younger versions of me and twenty younger versions of Micah—little people that looked nearly like our carbon copies. I guess I was the only *me*, I sometimes had to remind myself.

We were the Alphas—the first ones that survived. Other versions before us hadn't made it past infancy, but for some reason, we stuck and continued growing when others did not.

Even though it was the only thing I'd ever known, it was strange to see younger, identical versions of yourself, replicated many times. Each looked slightly different from the next, depending on what they ate, drank and how much they exercised each day. These stats were carefully tracked by Titus, True, Gareth, and the scientists.

Micah and I were the oldest by a few years. The others ranged from three to twelve years old, and there was a nursery with even younger versions of us, tucked away in a corner area of the hangar. Gareth let us see them sometimes, and he also showed us the Creatures every so often, when we persisted. We couldn't talk to the scientists—about twenty of them, men and women, who lived full-time in the hangar—but we could see ourselves as babies, which was fascinating.

They were so cute, and the older ones toddled over whenever we walked into the large room where they were kept, each clamoring to be held. I liked playing with them and imagining what I was like at that age, before I knew what was going on and that I was very, very special.

One of a kind, and the first of our kind to thrive. Gareth reminded us of this often, and I felt the weight of pleasing him on my shoulders with everything that I did. I wanted to prove we were the best version of ourselves, and that we couldn't be replaced.

"What are you thinking about?" I asked Gareth, as we watched the Littles.

His face was stern, but his mouth turned up in a smile when I asked.

"Oh, just thinking about the plans I have for you. For all of you," he said, staring at me with his warm, brown eyes. He had a way of looking through me, like he knew what I was thinking before I even did.

"What is it? Does it involve the Praeclarus side?" I couldn't help but ask. It was worth a shot. "Or . . . the outside?" I asked hopefully, feeling bold in the moment. I was dying to experience the real world.

"We'll see about that, my dear Delphine. We'll

see. But, you won't stay in the Triangle forever, I promise you. That would be a waste."

"Okay Gareth," I said, standing up to give him a hug.

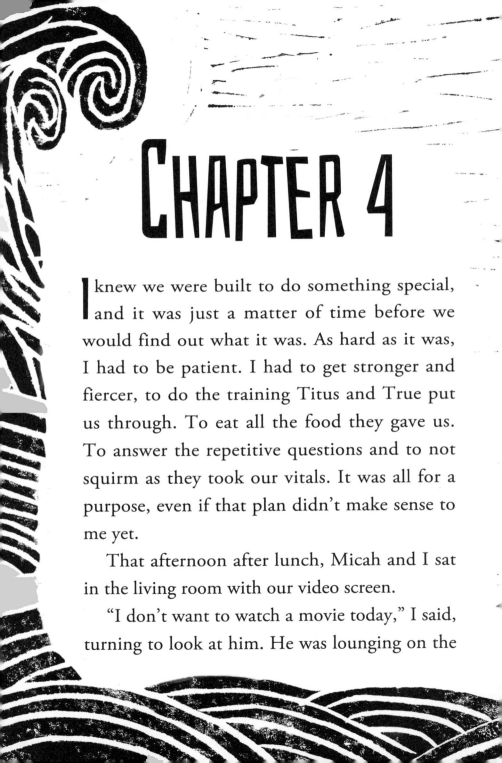

CHAPTER 4

I knew we were built to do something special, and it was just a matter of time before we would find out what it was. As hard as it was, I had to be patient. I had to get stronger and fiercer, to do the training Titus and True put us through. To eat all the food they gave us. To answer the repetitive questions and to not squirm as they took our vitals. It was all for a purpose, even if that plan didn't make sense to me yet.

That afternoon after lunch, Micah and I sat in the living room with our video screen.

"I don't want to watch a movie today," I said, turning to look at him. He was lounging on the couch next to me, freshly showered and smelling strongly of soap. "Can we talk?" I asked.

"Sure, what's up?"

"Why do you think Gareth created us?" I asked, trying my best not to sound upset. Micah was always so happy-go-lucky, while I got sad sometimes for no reason at all. The sadness bothered me—it felt less than perfect—and I did my best to push it away, but today it was lingering.

"I have no idea, Delphine. We have to trust his plan for us." He reached out his hand and I put my small palm in his.

"I know, but do you think we are *really* human?" I felt silly asking, but he was the only person I had to air my weird, unsettling thoughts.

"Stop it, Delphine. I hate when you talk like this. You know that."

"I can't help it," I said. I felt human. I felt emotions, like the people in movies. I felt joy when Micah made me laugh. I felt anger when Titus and True pushed us too hard during training and I felt

the urge to strike them, to punch them in the face, to kill them even, sometimes. These were all human reactions to things. Still, I couldn't help but question.

But maybe the questioning was what made me human the most.

Recently, we had learned something bad and it was shaking me up. When I was complaining during training, Titus told us out of the blue there were two kids on the other side of the hangar and that one was Gareth's daughter. True shot him an angry look and warned Titus to not say any more about it, but this news struck me like a rock flung at my chest. I couldn't breathe. Was I . . . jealous? I thought that was what it must be, even though I didn't understand it.

Why were they able to roam free over there, while we were stuck here?

Was it because Gareth viewed us differently? Like a science experiment? These thoughts marched back and forth in my head whenever I'd try to sleep.

"You have to stop," Micah said, pulling me in for a hug against his warm, bare chest. I felt my face flush and my body got hot instantaneously. He held me tight and wouldn't loosen his grip.

Tears brimmed in my eyes, and I brushed them away quickly, embarrassed.

"Why would you even question?" Micah asked, touching my wet face with his fingers and loosening his hug to pull back and look at me in the eyes.

"I don't know," I sniffled, feeling dumb for second-guessing everything when Micah was so sure and easy-going.

"I can prove that you're one hundred percent human," he said, his face serious. "Come here," he continued, and he wrapped his arms around me and pulled me in, kissing me hard and long on the lips.

"Woah!" I pushed him away, shocked. We'd never done this.

I had wondered what it would be like all the time. Usually when I was trying to sleep, my thoughts would turn to fantasizing about sneaking into his room. And I'd imagine having the guts to kiss him, but I never could muster the courage in real life.

It felt amazing. Better than what I could ever even hope, and my whole body buzzed, like it was electrified.

I felt silly for pushing him away when kissing him was what I wanted most of all. "Do it again," I said, and he leaned in and we kissed again and again.

There would be no movie today and that was just fine by me.

I felt alive. And he was right—when we kissed, there was no doubting that I was a real girl, through and through. My whole body felt it.

After a while, we lay back on the couch and were quiet.

"We have to trust Gareth. He has a plan for us." Micah said.

"I know. You're right. I don't know why I question things sometimes. I know it's foolish."

"It's not foolish. It's human," he said with a laugh.

"And when it's time for our next act, we'll be ready to prove to him that we belong here," Micah continued, squeezing my hands tightly in his, and staring at me so intensely, I almost felt embarrassed.

"That we're the best version of a human," I said, repeating what we'd been told many times before.

"Because he designed us," Micah said, finishing the mantra.

"Exactly."

We'd gone over this a million times, and tonight, it really felt true.

CHAPTER 5

Delphine – Age 15

Gareth approached Micah and me as we sat and watched old movies in our living quarters at the Triangle.

"So it's time we let you out of your cage, so to speak," Gareth said, gesturing at our surroundings. He smiled at us, waiting for a response.

"What? Are you messing with us?" I asked. I didn't want to be disappointed.

"What are you talking about, Gareth?" Micah pressed, standing up and folding his arms across his chest. He appeared serious, but I saw the twinkle of excitement in his eyes.

"You know Jorge, right?"

We both nodded. Jorge was the only Praeclarus member allowed in the Triangle—ever. Several years ago, Gareth first brought Jorge to our training field, where he observed us for many hours on end, every day, for many weeks.

Jorge was a world-famous guru of some sort, and Gareth's right-hand man. Since that initial visit, he returned about six times a year to see how we were developing. When we pushed Titus to explain why, he just shrugged and told us we needed to mind our own business.

After training, we showered and Gareth asked us to meet him and Jorge in our dining room. We sat down at the large, wooden table and Gareth looked like he had something very important to discuss.

"I finally have the news you've been waiting for."

We waited, excited. I grabbed Micah's hand under the table and squeezed it. "So . . . ?" I asked, feeling impatient.

"Jorge and I have identified a very special person that we need you to help bring to the island."

"You mean, we'll get to leave?"

"Yes. Not for good, of course. But for this special trip, yes," Gareth said, smiling wide at us.

"Really?" I asked, feeling my heart start to race. This was even better than I had hoped it would be. "But why send us? Don't you have others to do these sort of jobs?"

"Yes, but this is a high-stakes operation and I need to send people that I trust implicitly . . . which leaves the two of you, plus True and Titus."

"They'll come along?"

I tried not to sound disappointed, and Micah kicked my ankle under the table, frowning at me. "I mean, they'll come along?!" I repeated, faking excitement.

"Trust me, you'll need their assistance on this one. And, they'll be there to keep tabs on you. This will be a good test for both of you—of your loyalty, and how you behave under pressure," Gareth explained.

It sounded like the most exciting thing that might ever happen to me, and I nodded eagerly.

"And, if you don't succeed, there's always more of you, right?" he said, nodding toward the living area, where the Littles were being held. Gareth laughed, but eyed us sternly.

I knew he liked to mess with us, to see how'd we respond to his words, and I betrayed no response to this joke at all, just like I'd been trained.

I was more than up for the challenge. It's what I'd been waiting for. We needed to prove to Gareth that he got us right.

"We'll succeed, right Micah?" I asked, eyeing him.

"Of course. We were born to succeed," he replied, and I believed him.

"So, what is Ship Out?" I asked, not understanding.

Jorge and Gareth sat in front of us at the rough

wooden table in our dining room. True and Titus hunched over the opposite heads of the table, quiet and listening. True had a sour look on his face, to the surprise of no one.

"It's a program for loser kids. Criminals and druggies. Kids that won't be missed . . . much . . . " Gareth said. "I need more kids for the island anyway, so it works out perfectly."

"Need more kids for what?" Micah asked, and I caught Titus and True exchanging quick glances across the table.

Gareth ignored the question and kept on talking, "I'll get eight of them in one fell swoop. Most will be collateral damage, so we can snag Reed without arising suspicion. This is a solid plan. I wish I could take credit for Ship Out, but that's all Jorge."

Jorge sat there in his green, shiny caftan, listening and nodding along with Gareth's every sentence.

"I'll plant the Ship Out seed with his father,

Tim Mackenzie," Jorge said. "Reed is already a mess, trust me, so all we need to do is push him over the edge and I'm certain Tim will take the bait. He relies on my advice. I built my relationship with Tim carefully over many years just to get to this moment—to help you."

"And that's where you come in," Gareth said, looking at me. "You'll be the lure to draw Reed away."

"Me? How?" I asked, not understanding.

"We'll make sure his parents think he's a violent, blackout drunk on the verge of getting arrested or killed, and voila!"

"I don't get it . . . " Titus said, scratching at his chin methodically.

"We'll give Tim the ammunition he needs to make sure Reed is put on that ship, per Jorge's strong recommendation," Gareth continued, and he sounded a little impatient that we all didn't fully understand what he and Jorge had obviously been plotting for a while.

Titus suddenly smiled widely. "And the ship's where I come in?"

"Yes. I knew your sailing background would come in handy sooner or later."

"Later is the correct word, but I'll take it. Sounds like an adventure," Titus said. He'd been on the island for many years and was one of Gareth's most devoted employees. I'm sure he was a lot more stir-crazy than me, especially since he had to spend so much time in the Triangle, monitoring us instead of enjoying all the riches available on the other side of the island.

"But what about me?" True asked, confused.

"You're the muscle to keep the kids in line," Gareth explained, and I couldn't help but snort. True never shied away from using violent tactics to ensure we did our training every day. He'd be perfect.

"Years of practice with these ones will come in handy," Gareth said, gesturing to us. "Remember, these Ship Out kids are going to be the dregs of society. They have little to no discipline, from what we've gathered in their applications. They *need* to be whipped into shape—and you're quite good at that. So do what you have to do—or even what you want to do. Just keep them alive."

True's frown lessened slightly and he nodded. "Okay, I understand."

"But, where'd the other kids come from?" Micah asked, leaning forward on his elbows. He was so cute, I got distracted for a moment looking over at him. I was excited to be alone with him later tonight so we could celebrate this amazing new development together.

"Well, that's all Jorge's doing. He's a master of the long con, this one," he said, reaching out and slapping Jorge across the back. "He created Ship Out months ago, made a very fancy website, put some important-sounding referrals on it, and added a twist of new age mumbo jumbo—the stuff that Tim just eats up, by the way. And then, as the old adage goes, *if you build it, they will come*," Gareth said, smiling at Jorge.

"Yeah, families started coming out of the wood-work, looking for help—desperate for it. More families than we could possibly accommodate on the ship, which surprised us," Jorge explained. "It could almost be a new business venture."

"If it wasn't so fishy that the ship disappears," Gareth interrupted. "I'm afraid the ship crashing is going to put poor Dr. Wingett and Ship Out under water."

"Out of business," Jorge said, and they both laughed.

"So it's all fake? Who is Dr. Wingett?" I asked, my eyes wide. This sounded like a cool plot from a spy movie.

"A figment and nothing more," Jorge said, pushing his hands through his thick black hair and leaning back in his chair, smiling widely.

"But . . . why would you go through all of the

trouble?" Micah asked. "It seems like a whole lot of work to grab some kid."

"Oh yes, it is. But, this isn't *some* kid to me. It's a very special kid. Or, rather, the very ordinary kid of a very special person that's had it coming for many, many years. But it will be worth it," Gareth said. "And this way, his parents won't be searching for him when he disappears. They'll think he's sobering up out to sea. It'll be three months before they realize something's amiss."

Titus perked up even more. It was the happiest I'd seen him look in a while. "We're going to be gone for months?"

"Yes, and then once we ensure all of you are back on the island, we'll make sure the boat sinks in an unfortunate summer storm . . . it's tragic . . . "

"Why would you do that?" I asked, wanting to make sure I understood the intricacies of what they were proposing.

"Well, dear, Tim Mackenzie is a very rich and

resourceful man. If he knew that his only surviving son was still alive, I'm certain he'd devote all of his resources—both financial and technological—to saving Reed."

"Even though they don't get along, and Reed acts like an ungrateful twit more often than not," Jorge added.

"Yes, well, a parent's love is unconditional," Gareth responded, reaching out and placing his hands over ours. I always liked when he referred to himself as our father.

"So, what are you going to do with Reed when we bring him here?" I asked. Why would Gareth want this specific kid on the island?

"I'm going to make him pay for his father's transgressions, and do it publicly, for all my friends who also have a distaste for Tim Mackenzie and what he represents," Gareth said, laughing, and Titus and True chuckled as well.

"You'll see what I've been cooking up, I promise you, dear," Gareth said, assuring me.

"We'll get to see the Praeclarus side of the island when we get back?" I asked.

"Yes, that's precisely what I'm telling you, as long as you bring the boy to me safely and in one piece."

"Or, mostly one piece?" True interrupted, smirking and raising his eyebrows. He really liked to fuck with people.

"You have my permission to do what you need to do to keep those kids in check," Gareth said.

"So, when do we leave?" Micah chimed in.

"In a week. We have to get the ship prepped, and ready the final sailor with his duties," Gareth explained.

"Why do you need a third sailor, anyway?"

"Well, we need someone who knows the nuances of this particular boat, as it's a different model than what Titus and True are used to. They'll need a mate to help run the ship during the long journey," Gareth explained.

"We've found someone, actually," Jorge said, "but we have to make sure he's up for the trip."

"Who is it?" I wondered if it was someone else from the island I hadn't met yet.

"He's a believer in all the new age crap," Gareth said. "So, it's just making sure he has the disposition to be stuck with a bunch of bratty kids and these two on a boat for days and days on end," pointing to Titus and True. "Not an easy task."

"We should be ready by then. He's meeting the group in California," Gareth explained to Titus and True. "And he's a real pushover, according to Jorge. He'll make sure the vessel is running, but other than ensuring it stays afloat and gets back here, you'll have complete control over the Ship Out program and what happens on that boat."

Titus and True smiled at each other, and Titus reached out and shook Gareth's hand. "I know what a big deal this is. And how much you must trust us to let us leave. Thank you, sir, for this opportunity."

"I've trusted you for years with these two and all the young ones. I have no doubt you're the best of the best."

Titus smiled, looking thrilled to receive such glowing remarks.

"And you too, True. Of course." Gareth said, but it sounded like an afterthought to me and I saw True's frown return. He had a major inferiority complex. It was cringe-worthy to watch him when Gareth doted on Titus, which was the normal dynamic between the three.

After we were done talking, Gareth let us return to our living quarters and Micah and I collapsed on the couch, staring wide-eyed at each other.

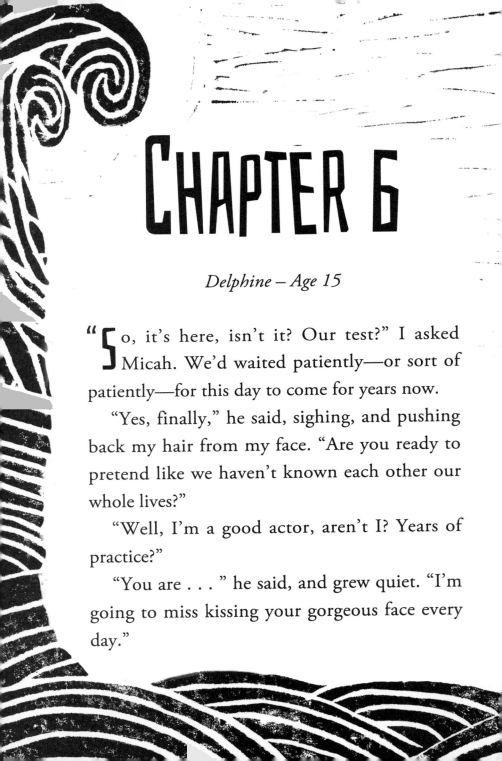

CHAPTER 6

Delphine – Age 15

"So, it's here, isn't it? Our test?" I asked Micah. We'd waited patiently—or sort of patiently—for this day to come for years now.

"Yes, finally," he said, sighing, and pushing back my hair from my face. "Are you ready to pretend like we haven't known each other our whole lives?"

"Well, I'm a good actor, aren't I? Years of practice?"

"You are . . . " he said, and grew quiet. "I'm going to miss kissing your gorgeous face every day."

"Well at least we'll still be together," I said. "And I'll sneak a kiss when no one's looking."

"You promise?"

"I don't think I can keep my hands off you for months," I said, smiling up at Micah and pulling him on top of me.

My whole body trembled with excitement and I doubted I could wait another week. I couldn't believe we'd be leaving. Not only the Triangle, but the island altogether.

We'd be on a boat, and feel waves underneath us for the first time in our lives, and experience the sensation of being un-tethered from the island. We'd feel salt water whip onto our faces, and step on foreign land, and I'd meet other kids, and see and experience so many other things I'd dreamt of but that I'd never seen.

Gareth trusted us completely. He wouldn't do this if he didn't expect us to follow through and bring Reed to him without incident.

I wondered why he'd send us if we were

supposedly so valuable and loved. I tried to push that thought out of my mind, but it noodled back.

"What do you think . . . " I asked Micah. "Are we going because we're replaceable? With the Littles and all . . . "

"What do you mean?" he interjected sharply. "Stop talking like that. We're going because he believes in us and our abilities. He'll let us leave the island and do this for him. To bring Reed to him."

"It's not because we're expendable?" I asked. I knew I shouldn't utter it out loud, but couldn't help myself.

"We're his most prized creations, Delphine. He tells us that all the time."

"I know, you're right."

But if that were actually true, wouldn't he not want to risk us being let off the island? I kept that thought to myself.

Ultimately, I was thrilled about the trip and couldn't wait to leave. When I rehashed my questions in my head, I realized my doubts were unwarranted. Gareth always did right by us and made sure we were okay.

I got excited thinking that there'd be a reward when we returned. I'd finally get to see the Praeclarus side, the part of the island I dreamt about.

We spent the next week getting the ship ready, filling it with food and supplies for our journey. It was a plain, unassuming vessel. Titus was nice and packed lots of special desserts from the Praeclarus dining hall, where they had real chefs that made pies and cakes and brownies for the guests every day.

I spent my last day watching the Littles train in the yard. I couldn't help but have the sneaking feeling they were advancing faster than Micah and I had—getting better at fighting each other at a quicker pace. Even the six-year-olds were wrestling like they'd been doing it their whole lives—and they had, I realized. Wrestling was taught beginning at age two.

I wasn't sure why they were progressing more quickly, but it made me uneasy—was it their training, the way they were fed, or how they were treated? Or, were there slight genetic tweaks in play, implemented with each copy of us that was created?

I wondered if we were being sent off to sea because these kids could easily take our place. They were nice enough and treated Micah and I with respect, but I kept my distance from the older ones. They made me feel uneasy.

Micah was buddies with several of the Littles, and he got a kick out of having conversations with them and seeing how they were similar to us, and how they were different.

He liked to tell me that their personalities were eerily similar to ours—at all ages—and he thought it was funny. On our departure day, we went to their living quarters one last time.

"We're gonna make all of you proud," he said. "Don't you worry about us."

"We're not," said #2 Girl, as I called her. Her real name was Duae. We all had separate names to Gareth and the staff, but in my mind, she was Number Two, second in line in terms of experience, and more importantly, Gareth's second favorite.

They all walked out to the dock as we got on the boat. All forty of them lined up, different in height but looking like slight variations of me and Micah at different moments in time. The Delphine Littles all grinned at me as we stepped on the deck, waving at me in unison. And the Micah Littles looked serious, but smiled back widely when Micah waved to them.

"Be good, boys!" he yelled out to them, and the little boys and girls giggled.

Titus and True stood behind us as Gareth and Jorge approached the boat.

"Looking forward to seeing you back here safe

and sound in several months. I'll be in close communication with you two," he said, nodding to Titus and True. Titus reached down and shook Gareth's hand firmly.

"We'll bring him home, don't worry."

"I'm not in the least bit worried. You've never let me down before."

Jorge stood behind Gareth and gave us reassuring nods.

"I am so proud of the two of you," Gareth said. "You are in the midst of fulfilling your destiny," he said, and I felt one tear bead up in the corner of my eye, and wiped it away hastily.

"Thank you, Gareth," I said. "We will show you we're worthy of this task."

As we untied from the dock, I grabbed Micah's hand and squeezed it tightly. We looked back at the island as we floated away from it. We had a long journey ahead of us—from this boat to a helipad to a private airport on a distant island to another boat. There were many precautions taken to get people to and from the island without detection from the outside world.

As we floated away, I could finally see the island for what it was. It was very green, with a long stretch of beach and hills that rolled up from the sea. I knew that just over those mountains, a whole amazing world was built solely for Praeclarus, and I couldn't wait to get back and see it for myself.

But for now, I felt happiness as the wind blew my hair back, and Micah pulled me in for a tight hug as the boat started to rock underfoot. We didn't even try to hide our relationship anymore, and nobody seemed to mind that it was developing. They granted us that happiness, a reprieve from the monotony of the Triangle.

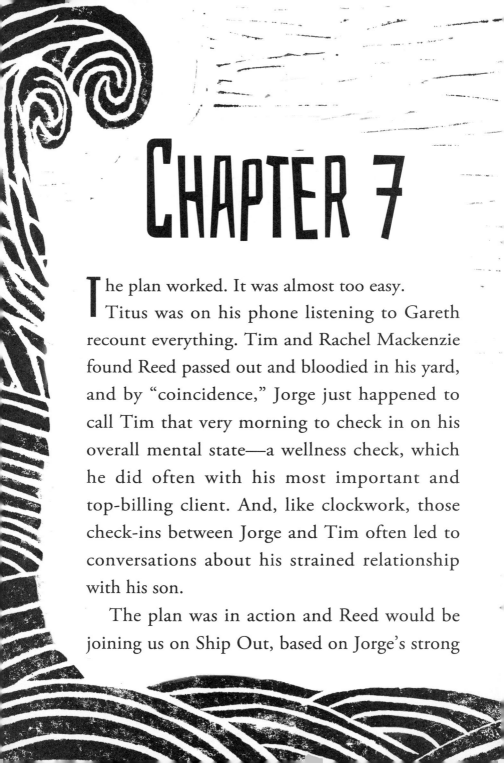

CHAPTER 7

The plan worked. It was almost too easy.

Titus was on his phone listening to Gareth recount everything. Tim and Rachel Mackenzie found Reed passed out and bloodied in his yard, and by "coincidence," Jorge just happened to call Tim that very morning to check in on his overall mental state—a wellness check, which he did often with his most important and top-billing client. And, like clockwork, those check-ins between Jorge and Tim often led to conversations about his strained relationship with his son.

The plan was in action and Reed would be joining us on Ship Out, based on Jorge's strong recommendation to Tim that he needed to take firm and definitive actions to save his son's life, and Jorge had just the program to recommend. He'd heard only the very best about it.

How he said that with a straight face is beyond me, but I admired the plan and how it unfolded so perfectly.

After getting confirmation that Tim took the bait, we got on the last boat that would take us from Reed's home in Oregon to San Diego, where the Ship Out boat would launch.

Before the departure day, we holed up in a gorgeous house overlooking the ocean; it belonged to a Praeclarus member who let us borrow it for a few days. It had floor-to-ceiling windows overlooking a cliff and the beach far below.

"You want to go for a walk?" Micah asked me the morning before Ship Out began.

I looked over at Titus and True, who were studying a large map of an ocean they had unfolded on the dining room table. They were discussing

something intently, and Titus stopped to look at us. He nodded approval.

"Be back in an hour, and don't talk to anyone."

"Of course," I assured them and smiled widely at Micah. "Let's go."

We stepped outside and the warm, sunny air felt amazing. Micah and I walked hand-in-hand down the steep wooden stairs to the beach, and as we got to the bottom, I let go of Micah's grasp, kicked off my shoes, and skipped ahead toward the water, the wind whipping my hair behind me.

I looked back and Micah was jogging after me, his dark hair shining in the sun, and grinning. We were free for just a moment. I realized we could start running and just not come back.

I didn't *really* want to do that, though. Where would we go? And what would we do? Our life was created for the island, and the Triangle was all we'd ever known. We were grown and taught to serve Gareth. That's all we could do.

When I got to the water, I stopped and braced

myself as the cold waves came in and rushed around my ankles before rolling back again.

I loved the sensation and it reminded me of the many, many days Micah and I had stood on the beach on the Triangle, gazing out at the horizon and talking about the outside world and how it was a complete mystery, except what we saw on our TV.

"It's funny being here, isn't it?" I asked, looking up at Micah, who now stood behind me and wrapped his arms around me. He bent down to rest his chin on my shoulder.

"Yeah, it's amazing. I'm loving every minute of it. But even still—and I can't believe I'm even admitting this—I'm anxious to get back."

"Me too," I said, relieved. "It's beautiful here, but honestly, after seeing those kids at the party in Oregon, I realized that *I am* different. And so are you. We'd never fit in out here."

"I know," he said, actually sounding sad, which was a tone I had never heard from him. The melancholy in those two words upset me, but I didn't respond.

"We can pretend we're just like them. We can pretend to have the same interests, but really, we're entirely different."

"I know, but that's because of our upbringing, not our genetics," Micah said.

I wasn't sure.

"I'm going to miss you," I said suddenly, and turned around and rested my forehead against his chest.

We both stood there, our skin pressed against each other, for what felt like an hour, and didn't say a thing.

We'd still be together on the boat, but we'd have to pretend like we were strangers, from different places entirely.

We'd rehearsed our backstories on the long journey to Oregon, asking question after question of each other about what we liked, what we didn't like, where we were from, and what our big sob story was that led to us being put on the Ship Out boat.

I'd have daddy issues. I loved old movies from the nineteen-eighties (this part was true) and could recite film quotes with an encyclopedic memory (also true, but just because of how many times we'd watched the same movies). I'd be a flirt and win Reed's trust over time, using my sarcasm and wit to make him like me.

"Oh . . . and I tried to kill myself, but I'll be coy about it," I said, the final detail in my character study. "But in case anyone notices my scars, I'll have an excuse."

Micah laughed at this choice. "You'd never do that."

"Of course not," I said, shaking my head emphatically. I wasn't sure if I'd have the guts. And where would my soul go, I wondered? Were the Littles' souls the same as mine—replicated? And if that were true, who would really miss me, besides Micah?

I'd *never* do that to Micah, either. We were each other's other half. It's the way it had always been and the way it would always be.

Micah's backstory was that he was the cool kid. The kid everyone loved. The one that gained everyone's favor and trust by being the type of person that put others at ease. The one who smiled widely and laughed easily. This really wasn't a stretch—at all. He could easily pull off being the popular kid.

He was very tall, with broad shoulders and dark skin, and a wash of thick hair that he pulled back out of his face. He was incredibly muscular—because of high school football, he'd say—not because of years and years of regimented physical training in the Triangle. Our stories held up.

"Are you ready? We better get back," Micah said, staring deeply into my eyes, and I nodded.

It was inevitable. A new chapter in our journey would start tomorrow. We'd have to be more self-sufficient. I wasn't positive I was actually ready, but as we headed back, I remembered that this was

Gareth's wish, and we had to prove to him that we were worthy. *Not replaceable at all.*

The next morning, Titus and True got up and left before the sun rose. They had to head to the dock where they were meeting the new crew member, Sully, who they needed because he understood how to manage the Ship Out boat's navigation and computer systems better than Titus and True. Jorge assured them he'd be easy to mold—a real pushover.

We'd been instructed to wait for our 'parents,' who'd be coming to take us to the dock by noon. They were friends of Praeclarus and could be trusted completely, Jorge had assured us before we departed.

Micah and I ate breakfast and got in normal American kid clothes. I wanted to look cute, so I put on a tight tank top and small jean shorts. Micah laughed, glancing over at me.

"Nailed it!"

"Really?"

"Are you kidding me? Even though you're the only girl I've seen in the flesh, I know you're incredibly hot. The guys are going to love you. I'm gonna have to do my best not to get jealous."

We sat on the couch making out, getting in as many kisses as we could before we were forced to pretend to be strangers. I was distracted, though, and pulled away, feeling too nervous. Micah grabbed onto me and held me tightly. We were sitting there quietly when someone knocked on the door. I quickly jumped up and straightened my clothes and walked to the entranceway.

When I opened it, I saw an older man and woman, both dressed in neutral, shabby clothes and looking grumpy.

"Are you Delphine?"

I nodded.

"We're your parents," the woman said and reached out her hand. I shook it and tried my best to smile and be calm.

The man walked in and grabbed my suitcases,

which were propped against the entryway closet door.

I stopped to look back at Micah who gave me a little wave.

"I'll see you on the other side, love," he said.

"Totes," I said, already in character.

My "parents" and I walked out the door, and I got into an old, slightly smelly car as they stuffed my bags in the back. We didn't talk at all during the whole thirty-minute drive. I tried to start a conversation but they wouldn't respond and stared straight ahead.

Who were they? And how did they get here? And why did Gareth trust them not to blow our cover?

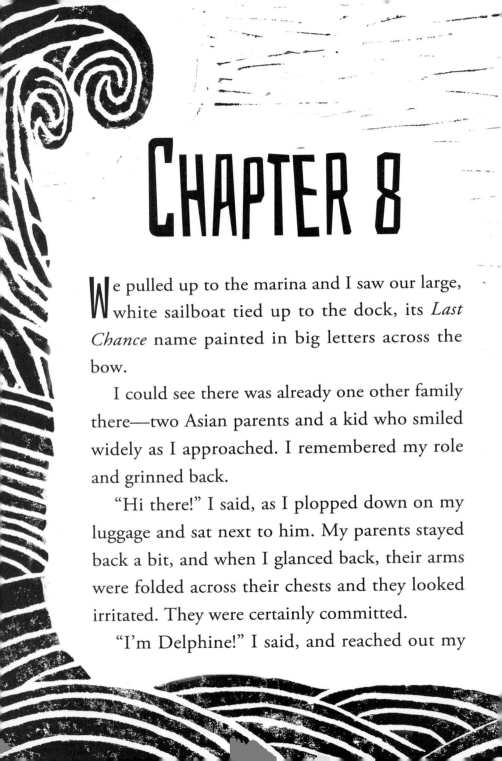

CHAPTER 8

We pulled up to the marina and I saw our large, white sailboat tied up to the dock, its *Last Chance* name painted in big letters across the bow.

I could see there was already one other family there—two Asian parents and a kid who smiled widely as I approached. I remembered my role and grinned back.

"Hi there!" I said, as I plopped down on my luggage and sat next to him. My parents stayed back a bit, and when I glanced back, their arms were folded across their chests and they looked irritated. They were certainly committed.

"I'm Delphine!" I said, and reached out my

hand. He shook it, looking relieved that I was friendly.

"I'm Benny. Nice to meet you."

"Great to meet you. Ready to have some fun?" I asked, tossing my hair over my shoulder, before putting it up in a sloppy top bun, and winking at him. He stared at me with his mouth wide open, like I had just blown his mind.

We sat there and waited for the others to show, talking about our lives back home—my fake life and his real life.

He was a really nice kid and I sort of felt bad that everything I said to him was a lie, but it was good practice. He seemed to buy every line I fed him, and I could tell he liked me by the way he looked at me eagerly, as if he wanted to make sure I liked him too. When I remembered we were basically kidnapping him, I couldn't really feel much guilt about giving him my fake backstory.

A few other families came and I met the other kids, one by one, introducing myself to each of

them, smiling with my perfect white teeth, and looking each person directly in the eyes when I talked to them. I laughed heartily at nearly everything that was said. I wanted everyone to be on my side, to trust me, and to long to be near me as we started our journey around the world to the island.

Micah came second to last. His "parents" looked nothing like him, which made me almost laugh out loud, but I kept a straight face and skipped over to him when he arrived, just like I had with everyone else.

"Hi, I'm Delphine," I said, stretching out my hand and pretending that we'd never touched. His skin was warm and it made me tingle all over.

"Micah. Pleasure is mine," he said, and I led him to where all the other kids were sitting. Their parents scattered behind them, some politely talking to each other, while others looked grim and stood by silently.

Titus and True were tending to the boat, and the new crew member, Sully, followed behind them, taking orders that Titus gave him. He looked like a puppy, anxiously obeying its master.

We waited, and I knew we were holding out for one more person. Finally, a slick-looking black car pulled up—much fancier than all the other vehicles—and Reed stepped out, along with his parents, who I'd also heard much about.

Reed's face had mostly healed, but I could see some bruising around his eyes and a cut across his nose.

Titus strode over to them, reaching out to shake Tim's hand. I couldn't hear their conversation from where we sat, but I could tell he was trying to impress Tim by the way he stood—chest out, head raised, and gesturing strongly at the boat and the group of kids.

As they approached, I worried for a moment that Reed might recognize me from the night of the party, but when I smiled at him, there was no hint of him remembering me. Instead, he looked surprised and embarrassed by my attention.

When he said goodbye to his parents, I knew it was the last time he'd see them. If Tim wasn't so bad, I'd maybe feel remorse for what we were doing. But knowing he'd crossed Gareth, he had to pay one way or another. Everyone did.

CHAPTER 9

Delphine – Age 10

"Now it's time to test how you respond to extreme temperatures," Titus said, pushing me toward the freezer. "Go in there. We'll come get you in a bit," he said, as he shoved me into a small, metallic room. It was lined with shelves stacked with frozen beef, chicken carcasses, and bags of cubed vegetables and fruits in bright oranges, reds, greens, and yellows.

I was wearing a tank top and shorts—nothing else.

"I don't want to!" I cried, feeling scared. *How long would I be inside?* "And what about Micah?"

I screamed, turning back to Micah who had tears in his eyes.

"He's next," True barked.

"Why can't he come in with me?"

"He has other testing to do," Titus said. "Now sit in there, quiet your mind, and it will be over soon enough."

He shut the door, and the room became pitch-black. It was cold and I felt around until I discovered the door handle. I pulled on it and nothing happened. I frantically searched for any other way to escape, but there was none. I realized I had no choice but to wait this out.

I sat on the ground, closed my eyes, and concentrated. *Be warm. Be warm. Be warm*, I repeated, and then I started to sing it to distract myself.

I was there for a very long time, willing myself to not feel cold. It was probably over an hour, and I concentrated hard on keeping my blood temperature steady.

Suddenly, I heard a clicking noise on my left

and I opened my eyes. It was still dark, but I could see two eyes watching me from a slit in the wall.

"Titus?" I called out.

A moment later, the door opened and the freezer was flooded with bright light and Titus and True pulled me out. Micah stood behind them, looking at me with a scared expression.

"Her skin is still warm to the touch and has retained nearly all of its color," Titus said, and True tapped furiously at his wristlet. I tried to see his notes, but he held it close to his chest and scowled at me.

Titus then thrust a thermometer in my mouth. A few seconds later, he pulled it out, glanced at it, then handed it to True, who read the number and laughed.

"What is it?" Micah asked.

"Oh, it's good news, don't worry. You and Delphine never cease to amaze us," Titus said, as he put down the blanket he had been holding. "I don't even think you need this."

"No," I agreed, feeling perfectly fine, physically, but furious that they had kept me in the freezer for so long, in the darkness. It seemed unusually cruel, even for them.

When Micah and I were alone later in the day, sitting on the beach, I asked him what happened.

"I don't know for sure," he said, as we lay back on the sand and let the water flow under our legs before it quickly disappeared back into the ocean.

"They made me sit in a tank of burning water for an hour—like a piece of chicken being cooked—and I feel fine."

"Really? Why would they do that to you?"

"I've been thinking about it a lot, actually. You know how in movies, people in the desert nearly die from thirst?"

"Yeah?"

"You ever wonder why that doesn't happen to us? All those hours we've spent out in the sun, getting our butts kicked all day, with no cover, and often with no water, either?"

"No." I'd never thought about it, and wasn't sure where he was going with this.

"We're not the same as normal people, Delphine."

"I know."

Titus, True and Gareth told us this all the time, but I didn't get it. Not really.

"They test us to see how we are different," Micah explained.

"I don't want to be different," I said. I wanted to be like the kids we watched in the movies. Normal.

"Oh, you do want to be different. I promise."

"Why?"

"We're special, Delphine. We're gonna do amazing things."

"Like what?" I felt impatient and wanted the amazingness to begin already.

"I'm not sure yet, but I know we have to be patient. They're training us to be stronger, faster, and less scared than regular-birthed humans.

Gareth has a plan for us, I just don't know what it is."

"Okay," I said, feeling disappointed that I just had more questions, but not wanting to harp on something that had no clear answers.

"Now can we go eat?" Micah asked. I was starving too, and we got up and went back to the dining room, where a lunch of sandwiches, strawberries, and a salad were waiting for us.

While we were eating, Titus came in and sat next to me.

"I'm sorry we had to put you in there."

"It's alright," I said, even though the truth was that I was mad. "I don't want to talk about it."

"I had to see how your body responds to freezing temperatures, and just like I expected, you passed with flying colors. It's very exciting watching you two grow," Titus said.

"Okay."

"You guys want a special treat?" Titus asked. I looked at him, wondering what he was suggesting.

"Is that a yes?" he asked, smiling at me.

"Yes . . . yes!"

Of course I wanted a treat. Titus and True took care of us, even if they did things I didn't understand. I had to trust it would all be okay.

He went out to the kitchen and walked back in carrying an impossibly tall cake. It was covered in a dark chocolate frosting and looked like it had been rolled in pecans.

"Where'd you get that?" I asked.

"From the Praeclarus side, of course. And there's more where that came from. If you're patient, you'll get to see it one day—I promise."

That's all I wanted—to experience the world that Titus painted for us through stories he told.

I fantasized about meeting the glamorous people that dressed in beautiful clothing—women that looked like Greek goddesses—and being treated to amazing long meals filled with every type of food I could imagine. I also dreamed of rooms filled with beautiful artwork from around the world, a place where wild animals like tigers and bears roamed, and where you could spend hours exploring the nooks and crannies of the hillside and miles of beaches.

I had to believe Titus that we'd end up there one day and that all this waiting around would be worth it. That prospect made me happy.

Whenever Micah and I explored the beach, we would always arrive at a tall rocky wall that stretched up into the sky, which was impossible to climb. It was lined with electric wire at the top and Titus told us that if we touched it, we'd be dead. If we could just reach the other side, we could see all the treasures and offerings that Gareth had created for his Praeclarus friends.

"You're a daydreamer," Micah always said, knowing that it was impossible to get over that wall.

"I can't help it. Aren't you?"

"No, not really. Things are pretty good here, all in all."

They were. He was right. We were special and lucky. I knew this in my heart to be true. I just had to repeat it to myself.

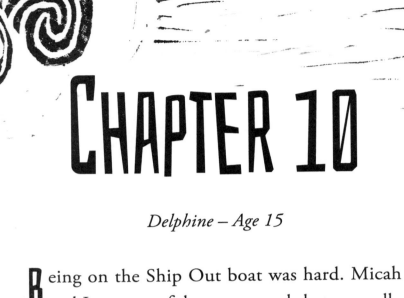

CHAPTER 10

Delphine – Age 15

Being on the Ship Out boat was hard. Micah and I were careful not to reveal that we really knew each other, or Titus and True. And we had to withstand the way Titus, True, and Sully treated us, which was even more miserable than usual.

I knew it was part of the ruse, but they really seemed to relish giving all of us a hard time and pushing us to our limits.

Micah played the sympathetic, defiant friend to Reed and the other kids, while I befriended Reed. I flirted with him shamelessly to ensure that he would trust me and that he'd confide in me with his secrets when we finally made it to the island.

We'd sit next to each other at dinner and I'd lean my head on his shoulder when Titus, Sully, and True weren't looking. I'd joke around with him to put him at ease.

Reed was a nice guy, and cute, and I almost felt bad that he was being punished for some ancient grievance Gareth had with his dad. But I pushed that thought away—Gareth wanted Reed, and so it would be done. Our helping enact the plan would just show Gareth that we could be trusted in any circumstances, no matter how bizarre or off-kilter it seemed.

The night the abduction was set to happen, Micah and I snuck into the bathroom together when everyone was prepping dinner.

It was a tiny space and we barely fit in it together, but we managed to close and lock the door.

He looked me up and down and kissed me hard, grabbing onto me and pulling me in. "I can't wait to be alone with you again."

"We can't be in here long," I sighed, wanting to stay but knowing it would be a problem if anyone came looking for us.

"Tonight's the night," Micah said. "Are you ready?"

"Of course," I replied. And it was true.

Before our trip, we'd talked over this part of the plan many times. We needed to act confused and angry, but ultimately go with it and convince everyone else that it was just part of the Ship Out plan to get "scared straight." We had to avoid the chaos that came from fearing for one's life. That would be Micah's job—to make sure everyone stayed in order and got on the lifeboat that would take us back to the island. If anyone rebelled, it could create panic, and we needed all the kids back on the island in one piece and alive—especially Reed. Gareth's orders.

I knew that night would be the evening we met the staffers who lived on the other side of the island, but didn't know about our existence. We couldn't let on who we really were. Gareth made that very clear. Aside from Titus, True, Jorge, and the hangar scientists, no one else knew about the Triangle and the experiments that happened over there; Gareth wasn't ready to share that just yet. We were to keep our secret for now and wait until he was ready for a grand reveal.

Gareth made us a deal. We'd get to be on the other side of the island—just like I'd always begged for—but we had to keep tabs on what was happening over there with the kids and with the staff. Titus and True couldn't be spies because no one would speak freely around them. More importantly, they had to get back to the Littles, who were currently being tended to by the hangar scientists.

CHAPTER 11

Delphine – Present Day

After Chelsea was taken away to solitary confinement, I stood up and looked down at myself. I had blood all over me—streaks of it covered my bare arms and my once-purple dress was now an inky, brownish maroon. I was sticky and tired and emotionally exhausted.

I'd publicly defied Gareth by jumping down in the ring to defend Reed. And I killed one his most prized creatures—one that must've cost millions to develop and years to grow to a fighting age.

The dead Komodo tiger was being lifted onto

a gurney by six large Suits. Its head flopped off to the side and its long tongue hung out like it was making a silly face at me, and I quickly glanced away, feeling regret for taking the animal's life. It was an innocent in this situation, born in a lab here on the island, and trapped in a cage its whole life.

When I was a younger girl, I'd visit the hangar and look at the creatures with Micah. It was like a field trip, and Titus and True and the scientists would stand behind us and laugh when one of the animals snarled at us or lashed out its claw against the metal of the cage.

I remember the malformed ones most of all—the animals with twisted legs that couldn't walk, so they'd drag themselves across their cages instead, howling in pain. I wondered why Gareth and the scientists didn't put those ones down, put a bullet in their head, or inject them with poison that made them fall asleep, and let them fade away.

"But aren't they in pain?" I would ask.

"Oh yes, that is obvious, just look at the

wretched ones. They both disgust and fascinate me. But we have to keep them alive—for science," Gareth reminded me. "It's about studying them so we can improve them, make the next iteration of this particular creature healthier, smarter, and stronger."

I felt a twinge of anger at this—he could be talking about me, and the Littles—even if he wasn't saying it outright. I bit my lip, considering whether or not to say something.

As I watched the Komodo tiger taken through the large metal gate, I guessed that there was another version of this creature in the hangar, ready to go.

As Suits led me through the exit, I refused to look up as the people in the crowd yelled down to me and laughed. I heard people screaming from all sides—they didn't know that I'd been on the island longer than any of them, that I was better and stronger than all of them. If I jumped up into the stands, I could kill any of them with my bare hands or with a flick of a dagger across their throats.

The Suits walking behind me escorted me to Gareth's quarters, where I had my own living space. My first night there, Gareth explained that he didn't like spending the *whole* night with the women who stayed with him and I scrunched my nose up, not wanting to hear about that.

When I walked in, Gareth was sitting on his bed, and he fixed me with an annoyed expression.

"You can leave us," he instructed, and the Suits behind us closed the giant gold door behind me.

"Go take a shower," Gareth said, "and then we'll talk."

I could tell he was seething by how little he said.

I wasn't looking forward to the conversation, but I knew I had acted in the way that was necessary to protect Gareth, and that's the angle I needed to take.

I got into the shower—it was lined with sparkly metallic tiles that gleamed under the room's yellow dome light. As the warm water ran over me, the blood and dirt washed off in streams and the pool at my feet ran from clear to bright red.

I sighed, enjoying the feeling and not really wanting to get out and face the music. Finally, I turned off the water, stepped out of the shower, and rubbed my face dry before I wrapped a warmed towel around me.

Looking in the mirror, I examined my face. I was unusual, a "pixie warrior," as Micah liked to joke with me. My skin was tanned but still had a splash of freckles across my nose and cheeks. My eyes were a bright green and I had naturally long, dark eyelashes. My hair was red, strong, and shiny. My body was lean and all the scars across my body healed to very pale golden stripes, nearly indecipherable unless you were up close and in natural light. And strangest of all, I had a perfect heart-shaped birthmark on my shoulder.

I put on the outfit that was sitting on the tall purple dresser in the corner of the bathroom. It was waiting for me—a pair of white shorts and a simple white t-shirt. Glancing in the mirror one last time, I knew that I was one of his most valuable assets. What's the worst that could happen?

I wished I could talk to Micah one more time, but I knew he was in the training camp and I couldn't speak to him privately.

I walked out into the sitting room, where Gareth was waiting for me. He was in an opulent, upholstered chair and wore a crisp linen shirt. He looked calmer than before—controlled, but I recognized this expression was hiding his anger.

"Sit down, my dear, next to me," he said, patting the chair beside him.

I did as he asked and then turned to face him. Before I could say anything, he slapped me hard against my left cheek with his open palm. The pain seared through me, but it was more shocking than anything else. He'd never done that to me before.

"Let me explain," I said, trying not to sound nervous.

I waited for him to interrupt but he sat there, staring at me with a tight-lipped expression. I tried to read what he was thinking.

"Yes, please do," he finally said.

"Reed's our insider to figure out what is being planned."

Gareth was quiet for a long time and then finally spoke. "We were going to nip the plan in the bud today, cleanly. If the traitors are trying to reach Reed's dad, we need to take Reed out of the equation right away."

"Reed trusts me, Gareth. He thinks I'm like him. He likes me. If you give me just even another week to have my ear to the ground, I can figure out what they're up to, and we can make sure that *all* of the traitors are taken care of, not just Reed. Killing him today would've been short-sighted."

I'd never spoken so plainly to him before, and Gareth looked both annoyed and ever so slightly amused.

"You made me look bad out there today,

jumping down to defend Reed. You killed my creature, and looked *too* good doing it."

"So?" I asked. "Doesn't everyone just want a good fight?"

"Yes, but not at my expense. And to disobey my command . . . it doesn't look good that my own 'lover' would make me appear so foolish."

"No, Gareth, you don't understand. That was part of my intention. I need *everyone* to think I'm on Reed's side. All the spectators. All the Suits. Ames. Elise. Everyone must think that I hate you, and that I'd do whatever it takes to help take you out."

Gareth sized me up, as if trying to weigh if what I said was the truth.

"Sometimes I feel like the number of people I can trust is dwindling. You are one of my most valuable allies, Delphine. You cannot defy me—do you understand?"

"Yes, I'm sorry Gareth." And I was genuinely remorseful.

"I don't know who to trust since my security system was hacked," Gareth said. "My video and audio surveillance is being scrambled every day now and we can't figure out how to bring it back to normalcy."

"What? How is that possible?"

I knew Gareth's security was top notch and I was shocked to hear that it had been compromised.

"The people in the security bank brought it to my attention. But I thought—what if it was one of them who tampered with it? I am not sure who to believe."

"That's why I'm here Gareth—to help uncover the truth. You can't just cut off the weed; you have to remove its roots completely. We need to see just how deep this poison is that could ruin the island."

He looked genuinely worried, which was something I wasn't accustomed to.

"If Reed is able to communicate with Tim Mackenzie, that will change everything. Somebody out there will be looking for us—someone with unlimited means and access to technology. It's a matter of time until we are found out, and then the fighting for the island's survival will get much more complicated and difficult."

He picked up his glass of whisky and swirled the ice cubes around with a flick of his wrist.

"I have to keep Ames, Elise, and Reed apart. I can't take any chances," he said.

"No. You have to give them opportunities to talk. And me and Micah too. Make sure it seems to them like you have no idea what's happening."

"That's a huge risk."

"I know, but we'll work quickly. Remember, you built us to be able to help you handle situations like this. To be your . . . family."

I paused, needing him to understand that I was truly on his side and that I wasn't going to screw him over.

This was the most vulnerable I'd ever seen him.

"I love you, Gareth," I said, for the first time in my life. He looked surprised, but he smiled and he reached out for my hand, which he squeezed tightly.

"Of course I love you too, Delphine," he said, and pulled me firmly over to him, forcing me to sit in his lap. I was stronger than him, but I didn't want to displease him by trying to move away.

He put his arms around me to hold me in a hard, long hug. His warm breath brushed past my ear.

"We can do your plan, but I must punish you in front of everyone for disobeying me."

"Okay," I said, accepting my fate as a necessary by-product of doing what was right to protect Gareth in the long run. "I understand."

"When it's happening, remember that I'll always love you. But if you ever disobey me again and make me look bad, I'll tie Micah to a chair and force you to watch my other Komodo tiger tear him apart. Then I'll strap you down to a board, and have him eat you from the feet up."

He released me from the hug, and looked at me with his warm smile.

Instead of feeling anger about his threats, I left the room determined that I'd prove to him that I was the best thing he'd ever made.

CHAPTER 12

The night of the Ship Out abduction, no one could find out that we were from the island, so we were drugged along with the rest of the kids.

After the kidnappers' speedboat arrived at the island, we were placed in the arrival holding cell for new fighter recruits. Titus had told us that would happen, but it was still jarring to wake up in a jail cell.

I knew Titus and True had to get back to the Triangle to check in on the Littles, so we wouldn't be seeing them again for a while, and we'd be in the hands of our new keepers.

"This is probably still part of Ship Out," I heard Micah say, and Reed agreed.

I stood up and felt groggy and unsure on my feet. I saw Rose, still passed out on her cot, and she was the only other person in the cell with me. Everyone else was stirring now.

"What's going on?" I called out to Micah and Reed, each in separate cells. We all faced a circular area in the center, and I knew someone would be coming to retrieve us soon. Gareth had outlined everything in detail before we left, and I was excited for the time when he'd release us so Micah and I could explore the Praeclarus side of the island freely, just like Gareth promised.

He said that he'd extract us as soon as he could without arising suspicions with his staff. In the meantime, we'd have to act dumb and go along with the rest of the kids.

As we waited, Micah was doing a good job playing the leader, assuring everyone as they woke up that this was all normal, and that we'd all be

heading back home soon—that the prison cells we were in were just an extension of Ship Out. We didn't want everyone to get at the truth yet—that would come soon enough—but for now, we wanted to keep everyone calm and cooperative.

It was laughable to me, pretending this was still a part of Ship Out, but everyone seemed to take the bait—reluctantly in most cases, but there wasn't another obvious answer.

Suddenly, the door in the center area swung open and a thin, pale man with light blonde hair and wire-rimmed glasses walked through the door. He was wearing a white outfit, and I immediately realized he was a Suit.

I quickly snuck a glance at Micah across the room and he smirked ever so slightly.

Titus had told us about the White Suits for years. They were Gareth's staffers on the Praeclarus side of the island. Everyone wore the same outfit, as Gareth liked the uniformity. On the Triangle side, Titus and True wore what they pleased, but whenever they crossed over, they had to change and appear like they were the same rank as everyone else, even if that wasn't the case. They were given unprecedented access to both sides of the island, so they were special. True liked to remind us of this fact all the time.

The man introduced himself as Darby. He was very friendly and he humored bewildered questions from everyone before ordering more Suits to bring us food.

I was ravenous after eating horrible bland mush on the boat for two months. I wanted to gobble this all down right away, but I had to pretend to be hesitant, like the others, who didn't understand why they'd been drugged. Finally, after Darby tested the food for himself, I felt it was okay to eat. I scarfed down everything so quickly I nearly choked.

Afterwards, I sat down on the bed and couldn't help but sneak glances at Micah when I thought no one else was looking. He was so handsome—I wanted to be free with him, to sit on the beach together, to explore the mountains we'd only seen from afar. He wouldn't look my direction and I realized that was probably for the best. I was supposed to be trying to win Reed's favor, not Micah's.

I felt Reed looking at me, so I glanced up, locked eyes with him, and flashed a worried smile. He was cute too, but didn't interest me in the least. I'd have to fake it and let him think he actually had a shot with me.

Once the last plate was practically licked clean, Darby ordered that we get dressed. He pulled a curtain around Rose's and my cell so the boys couldn't look in on us. As soon as the curtain was closed, Rose turned to me. She had a panicked look on her face and her hair was a mess.

"What's happening here? I don't think this is part of Ship Out!" she whispered.

Tears welled up in her eyes, and I stifled an annoyed sigh. I'd been forced to become close to her during the Ship Out journey. She was the only other girl in the program, and for some reason, that seemed to imply that we should be friends.

I really wasn't interested, though. I found her weak—she cried easily, she whined a lot, and she seemed to think her body was made of glass. Whenever Titus and True ordered that she do any physical work on the boat, she ended up sobbing loudly within minutes. It was tiresome.

So, with Rose standing before me on the brink of full-blown crying, I knew I had to ease her fears and calm her down. I pulled her into a hug. She was trembling.

"Shh . . . shh . . . Rose . . . it's okay. It's okay," I said, trying to act sympathetic like I'd seen people do in movies. "This is part of Ship Out. I know it is."

She sniffled and pulled her head back, looking at me hopefully. "How can you be so sure?"

"Well, promise not to say anything to anyone?" I asked, working quickly to come up with a believable lie just so I didn't have to endure her freaking out.

"Yes, of course. We're best friends!" she said.

"Awww . . . " I replied, thinking it was funny that she felt that way. "Yes, we are."

"So you can trust me one hundred and ten percent," Rose assured me.

"Okay, well . . . here's the thing. Titus told me this was going to happen. I think he kind of liked me and was trying to make me like him, so he told me a bunch of secrets about Ship Out. And this part of the journey—yes, he told me about this too. They're just trying to freak us out before we head back home."

"Well, it's working," Rose said, starting to calm down a bit.

"This is just a scare tactic, just like the rest of the shitty stuff Titus, True, and Sully have done to us. You're stronger than this though, right?" I asked.

"Yes!" she said, and sounded like she was

starting to believe it. She wiped at her nose with her hand.

"Okay, well let's get dressed." I handed her the small shorts and sports bra that were on our night-stand and quickly got myself dressed too. I didn't want her to notice the scars on my stomach and back. Even though they were almost unperceivable at this point, they were there and I was too tired right now to have to elaborately lie about my past as a suicidal cutter.

When we were done, Darby pulled back the curtain and I caught Reed quickly looking me up and down. I knew my years of training had chiseled my body into something guys desired.

Darby led us out into a hallway lit by torches. At the end, we arrived at a door that he opened, letting in blinding sunlight.

He ordered us to walk through and we found ourselves standing in a grassy, dirt-pocked field. It didn't look dissimilar to the field in the Triangle where Micah and I had trained every day of our whole lives—with the exception that this one was surrounded by sky-high stone walls on each side, with viewing windows that looked down upon us.

I glanced up and saw the dark shadow of someone standing in a window. I wondered if it was Gareth gazing upon us, seeing Reed for the first time, and checking in on Micah and me.

We'd been good. We'd held up our end of the deal. We'd stolen Reed from his home without actually "stealing" him. We'd kept tabs on Reed the whole boat ride and we'd been subjected to Titus and True's relentless abuse. We'd proven that we could be trusted with the most important of missions and that we'd succeed. Now it was time for him to let us out and for Micah and I to have some alone time together again.

I kept having to remind myself that we'd have to be patient.

Darby introduced us to Ames and Max and explained to us that they were our trainers to continue our path toward wellness and clean living.

Ames and Max put us through a series of super-easy tests to gauge our strength and agility—push-ups, jumping rope, wrestling, and the like—all mere warm-up exercises compared to the rigorous training that we'd been experiencing every day since we were young kids.

At the beginning of the session, Micah and I walked over to the drinking fountain together. It was on the far wall of the grassy area and no one else was within earshot.

"Act like you haven't been doing this every day for years," Micah said, as he bent down to get a sip.

"Of course," I agreed.

We'd have to look like we were weaker than we actually were, and so I pretended to get fatigued during the training when I was actually quite comfortable. I giggled as I tripped over my jump rope and it tangled in my feet. I collapsed to the ground after jogging around the perimeter of the track twenty times, even though I'd barely broken a true sweat.

Micah, the 'football player,' fared a little better, but I could tell that he was trying his best to look like a kid who had grown up in a 'normal' American setting—like a high school athlete rather than a finely-tuned warrior who had been conditioned nearly his whole life to fight.

We trained like that every day for two weeks and I kept waiting for Gareth to come release us. I knew he had a master plan in the works, but he hadn't shared that with us yet. Micah reminded me when we had our precious few seconds alone in the corner of the yard that we needed to keep the faith.

Everyone seemed in good spirits—I think because we were on solid land, eating delicious food every day, and because Ames and Max treated us firmly, but were nice. The kids talked about how we'd all be returning home soon, although Reed seemed more reserved than the others. He was the most leery.

One day while we were training, someone walked into the side viewing area. Shading the sunlight with my hand, I made out a girl about our age, but she was dressed in a flowy silk top and she was absolutely gorgeous—like a movie star, but even prettier. She had perfectly styled dark hair and tanned skin. I felt the collective air in the field disappear as everyone stopped to stare at her.

"Hello there," she called out to us.

"Welcome, Chelsea. Glad you can join us," Ames said in return. I looked over at Micah, who was staring at her with a dumb expression on his face.

Chelsea?!

So this was the girl I'd heard about from Titus—Gareth's daughter—the girl who was allowed to roam free, didn't have to train at all, and had the run of the island with her boyfriend, Odin.

I felt a jealous anger rise up inside me. I didn't know her, but I already hated her.

CHAPTER 13

Chelsea watched us go through various training exercises, but I wasn't sure why exactly.

She seemed smug to me, sitting there on a purple throne, cooling herself with a silk fan as we toiled in the sun. *How could she sit there and not feel bad for us? Why did she look like she enjoyed herself?*

I saw Micah head for the water fountain and I quickly followed him.

"Who does she think she is?" I hissed at him as he bent to the spout.

"Chelsea?"

"Yeah, why is she here anyway?"

Micah shrugged. "I dunno. Maybe Gareth will be here soon too?"

I sighed loudly, annoyed that he wasn't perturbed about her sudden appearance like I was. "I don't like—"

"Okay guys . . . time to start up again!" Ames yelled to us, and we turned and started to walk slowly back to where everyone else was standing. I saw Reed sitting in the group, sneaking glances up at Chelsea as she fanned herself while staring off in the other direction.

He appeared love-struck, and I was surprised that I felt a twinge of something that could only be described as jealousy.

Ames told us that we were going to grapple and he put Reed up against the sniveley kid, Marcus. Marcus disliked Reed for reasons none of us really understood, so it would be a good matchup. I wanted to see what Reed was made of when truly challenged.

Reed was trying to show off by talking trash as

he and Marcus squared off. I could see Reed positioning himself slightly toward Chelsea, as if he was making sure she got a good look at him. Reed took Marcus out easily. Marcus looked furious—like he wanted to kill him.

"That was no luck," Chelsea said, encouraging Reed even more. Ames ordered them to square off again to give Marcus another chance. I could tell that Reed was distracted by Chelsea by the way he kept glancing at her, which probably wouldn't end well for him. Lesson one in fighting is that you never take your eyes off your opponent.

Sure enough, as they sparred again, Reed glanced in Chelsea's direction and Marcus took him down. Reed's head cracked against the ground, hard. He passed out, but I knew he'd be okay. I'd had the same injury plenty of times during training. Ames called for a stretcher and a few Suits came to take Reed away. Marcus looked pleased with himself.

That night, while we were eating dinner, Ames came to see us.

"Delphine, there's someone who wants to talk to you," he said.

"Who?" I asked, looking up at him, trying my best to appear scared.

"I'm afraid I can't say," he said. "But it's been ordered."

"Am I in trouble?" I asked.

"I'm not sure," Ames said, shrugging. I got up from the table and glanced at Micah, who looked worried.

"Who is it?" Micah asked, playing into the narrative that we still didn't know what was going on.

"Afraid that's all I can share," Ames said, leading me out the door.

As we walked down the hallway, I glanced around, taking everything in. We passed men draped in outfits that looked like white sheets, their big, hairy chests and bellies pushing against the fabric. They stared at me as I walked by, and I heard them talking about me.

"Who is that?"

"A new one?"

I knew they were the Praeclarus members, here for one of their vacations—as Titus had described to us, "a vacation with no rules."

We got to a long corridor and I tried to ask again. "Where are you taking me?"

"To see Gareth," he said, not turning to look at me as he walked briskly. I kept in stride with him and tried not to step on the backs of his feet.

"Who's Gareth?" I asked, pretending to be confused and scared. "And why does he want to talk to me? I don't understand—" I asked, acting dumb. Ames couldn't have an idea who I truly was.

"He runs the island."

"But who is he? Is he in charge of Ship Out?"

Ames chuckled. "I guess you could say that."

I tried to play the confused girl I needed to be. "Why does he want to see me?"

"He wants to see you after I shared a little bit about you and how your training is going," Ames said, but I saw him shrug. "Not sure why, honestly—except for, you know, the fact that you're female—and attractive."

"What do you mean?"

"Gareth likes companionship," he said as we approached a set of large gold doors surrounded by large, potted palm fronds. He looked disgusted, but resigned to follow orders.

Gross, I thought. I was relieved that wasn't the real reason I was being brought here. I tried not to think about Gareth having sex.

As he buzzed the door, it swung open and Titus was standing there.

"Oh!" Ames said, obviously surprised to see Titus. "What are you doing here? I thought you'd been reassigned to manage the Reserve."

"I have." Titus wouldn't look at me when he

talked. "I needed to talk to Gareth about the animals. I have new ideas about how to control them. They're getting a little too comfortable and I think we need to lock things down," he said, and then turned his head toward me. "Now it's our little secret I was here, right?" he asked.

"Yes," I said, and Ames looked over at me, puzzled. "I'll be seeing you later, Ames," Titus said, and then walked out the door.

"That guy is an asshole," Ames said, as if he couldn't help himself.

"I agree. But, what is he talking about—animals?" I asked, looking around, trying to make sure Ames believed me that I was a complete innocent in this situation.

"This island is full of surprises. You'll see," he muttered, as if reminding himself too. "Now, follow me."

We walked down a long passageway that was covered in gold tiles. It was magnificent and I was thrilled to finally be there.

When we got to the entrance to the room, Gareth stepped around a corner—like he knew the precise moment we'd appear—and looked me over.

I was wearing the small sports bra and tiny white shorts.

"Mmmmm . . . " he said approvingly, then looked at Ames. "Good work, my friend. She'll do just fine. Now give me some time alone with her."

Ames nodded. "Yes, of course. I'm glad you're pleased," he said, bowing slightly before walking away.

Gareth closed the big doors behind Ames and turned to look at me. "Sorry about that, dear," he said.

"That's disgusting," I said, not liking the implication that Gareth and I were going to be lovers. He was like a dad to me.

"I agree, but I have to keep up appearances. I don't fully trust Ames anymore," he explained. "Now come in, we need to talk."

He walked me over to a sitting area with pretty

blue chairs and walls that were covered in a silvery-yellow wallpaper. There were framed pictures of him everywhere: standing over the carcasses of wild animals, posing with his arm around men, and sitting on the beach with a beautiful woman, with a little baby smiling up at the camera in the sand between them.

"So, what do you think?" Gareth asked, gesturing around the room.

"About your room?"

"About the island as a whole," he said, laughing.

"Well, I haven't seen very much of it yet," I responded, trying not to sound too disappointed.

"It will happen, I promise. You and Micah did a very good job bringing Reed and the others here safely."

"Thank you," I said. It never got old hearing him compliment me.

"You proved that you can handle complex assignments and follow through with loyalty," he continued.

"Of course," I said. Loyalty was one of the most important qualities a person could have. Titus had taught us that for as long as I could remember.

"I will let you see other parts of the island, but I need you to stay in the training area and have your ear to the ground, listening in," he explained.

"But I thought we'd be free once we captured Reed?" I asked.

"You will be, but I heard something tonight that disturbed me greatly, and I need your help for just a bit longer."

I stared at him, waiting.

"I have a staffer here named Elise that has been trouble for way too long. I should just get rid of her, honestly, but she's one of the best doctors and scientists on the island, and I like to keep her in my back pocket, just in case."

"Okay," I said, not understanding. "Why have I never seen her in the Triangle?" I asked. If she was the best, she'd be over there, helping the scientists with the Littles.

"She used to be stationed over there, actually," Gareth explained, "when you were very, very young. But she didn't agree with what we were doing . . . with you and Micah actually . . ."

"Me? What problem did she have with me?"

"She thought it wasn't moral to keep trying to create you. She thought the way we made you, in a lab, made you less than human."

That stung, and I felt my face turning red. "She said that? Even after she saw us?"

"Yes, she helped raise you when you were babies, and then she deserted you, leaving the Triangle and the Hangar for good."

I felt anger rise up against this woman. *She left us? She thought we weren't human enough? It wasn't our fault how we were created and born.*

"So what's this have to do with what you heard tonight?" I didn't understand.

Gareth leaned forward in his chair, looking at me seriously. "Elise was tending to Reed after his injury, and the way she was talking worried me."

"What do you mean?" I asked.

"I think she was telling him things she shouldn't, which makes me question her loyalty. I've long feared she might turn against me to escape the island."

"And how did you hear this?" I asked. I didn't understand.

"I have audio and video surveillance of almost the entire island. But my systems keep going down and coming back up—because someone is messing with the system. I got my audio back up tonight just as Elise was finishing talking to Reed. I only heard the very end of their conversation, but it made me wonder."

"And what does this have to do with me?"

"I need you and Micah to keep tabs on Reed and report to me if he tells you anything about Elise, and if she's planning something. And I'm going to need it to look like you're just another one of the kids. Completely."

"I understand," I said, even though I wasn't sure I knew really what was going on.

"So that means that you and Micah are going to be put into the Ring."

"The Ring?"

"The Coliseum."

"Titus told us you built that, but why? I don't understand," I said.

"For entertainment and to show off what I've been creating, eventually. I want you to fight against the other kids and take them out."

"Why?" I asked. I knew what take them out meant. During our training in the Triangle, we often were made to 'take out' animals like deer and rabbits. They wanted to confirm that we could kill without flinching.

"I'm testing you to see how you handle real fighting conditions, and your will to win."

"But why?"

"You may be the forefront of the future of

modern ground warfare, my dear, and I couldn't be more proud. You're exceeding all my expectations."

"Modern warfare?"

"I'm considering selling my clone technology to the highest bidder. It will revolutionize the way humans fight in the future," he said, looking at me eagerly.

I tried to process everything he was saying, but it didn't make sense to me.

"What do you mean?"

"No more sending our own children to fight wars. The government that buys my technology will be able to grow their own human army. They will be able to tweak their ground troops to be able to withstand certain conditions better—the cold, the heat, to be faster than their opponents, to see better in darkness, to be tougher mentally—all the things that make you superior to others."

"So I'm just an experiment to you?" I asked. I couldn't help stating the question that ran in my mind again and again.

"Not at all, my dear. You are the best version of a human that I've ever seen, and I can make you again and again. Your legacy will live on forever in the younger versions of you that exist in the future, on and on and on throughout time."

My mind reeled with this news. My first instinct was to be angry, but then I felt something closer to pride—that we were the first soldiers among many to come and that Gareth wanted to test us—not because he didn't love us, but because he trusted we'd be able to pass every test put forth better than a normal human ever could.

"Okay," I said. "I understand and I'm ready to prove myself to you—I'll do whatever it takes," I continued.

"I want to see you fight. For real. To see if you have the guts and disposition to kill someone that you've befriended without remorse or hesitation. Do you think you can do that?" Gareth asked.

"Yes," I said. "Who will it be?"

"Your dear friend, Rose."

I crinkled my nose, thinking about the weak girl. That would be an easy opponent.

"Simple."

"I know, but it's just a warm-up."

"Okay. So as long as I listen in on Reed's and Elise's plans and participate in these fights, you'll let me and Micah roam free eventually?"

"Yes, I promise," Gareth said, reaching over to shake my hand.

CHAPTER 14

After I killed Rose in the battle, I did feel something—I think it was pity. I tried to make the fight tougher than it was, as Gareth instructed. He said that the Praeclarus members always grumbled when the matches were over too quickly or if the opponents didn't put up enough of a battle.

I even let her stab me to increase the believability. I'd been stabbed by Micah accidentally before during our training and I knew my body would recover quickly. It hurt, but when I looked up at Gareth, I saw he was smiling widely. I did him proud.

After I healed from the fight, I was put in

a different training area—the elite barracks that separated the kids after arrival. The fighters were brought to this section of the island and the rest were made Suits. Titus came to talk to me and explained that I was being put in the area that Reed would be brought to after he recovered, along with Micah. I couldn't wait to see Micah again.

When I entered the training field, Ames was waiting for me.

"How are you feeling?"

"A little sore, but alright," I said. My wounds were wrapped in gauze, but were healing rapidly and felt fine.

"Ahh . . . who is this?" someone demanded, and I looked over. A very large, muscular kid walked up. He had a strange accent, a large tuft of brown hair, and a sneer on his face. He looked me up and down and smiled.

"This is Delphine, our newest recruit. One fight in and she did a good enough job, so here she is," Ames said, as more kids gathered around.

"Delphine, this is Odin. You'll find that he's a very large presence in this camp. Don't let him get under your skin."

I eyed Odin. I knew who he was—this was Chelsea's boyfriend. Titus and True had told me about him. I wondered what he had done to become a fighter instead of living freely with Chelsea.

"Delphine, huh? You are a little thing, aren't you? Like a hot little leprechaun," he said, leering at me. His friends that hung to his side laughed hysterically.

I shrugged. What an idiot.

"I've got my eye on you Delphine," he said, pointing at me.

"Whatever . . . " I brushed him off as I walked away.

"I'm going to keep my tabs on you Delphine—very closely," he called after me, and even though I wanted to turn around and punch him in the face, I knew I had to keep my cool.

The training in this area was tougher and the kids brutally beat on each other, each trying to prove their worth. They had all been in the Coliseum before, so they understood the stakes and were each fighting for their own life, even in training.

Reed came a few days later and I acted like I was absolutely thrilled to see him.

Then, when Chelsea appeared in the stands to watch us, I saw Reed smiling up at her, which infuriated Odin.

Chelsea seemed to command every boy and man's attention whenever she walked into an area, which made Odin visibly angry.

Reed kept on looking at me throughout the day—as if he had something important he wanted to say to me—but there was nowhere to go to speak privately. I needed to figure out a way to hear if he'd learned anything about her plans to escape.

At the end of the day, everyone was exhausted. We were covered in dirt, blood, and sweat. I tried to hang back to talk to Reed before dinner, but Ames pushed me ahead so he could chat with Reed instead.

That seemed fishy to me, but I pretended to shrug it off.

I headed to the dining hall, where I positioned myself at the far end of the long wooden table, where Reed could sit next to me and we'd have some room to talk freely.

I knew Gareth wanted me to ask about Elise, but I'd been thinking about Chelsea and how she looked at Reed. Could Chelsea be flirting with him? I couldn't take the chance that she might do something that would limit my access to him.

"What's up between you and Chelsea?" I asked. I decided to play the angle that she might be able to help us. She knew the island, after all. I watched his response. Would his face betray anything? I saw him flinch ever so slightly—there *was* something there.

"Aha! You like her don't you?" I said, nudging him in the shoulder.

"No, that's not true," Reed responded quickly, but his voice raised a little and I knew the truth immediately.

"Oh, don't be embarrassed Reed. You should try to get as much info as you can out of her. She must know a way off the island, right?" I asked, trying to sound supportive and not like I was accusing him of something.

"Maybe? She says she does, but I also wonder if she's just messing with me," he said, looking at me.

I took a big bite of pie, not wanting to reveal that this was exactly what I was hoping to hear.

I tried to make light of this news, to not seem like I was excited.

"Nah. You should totally hit and quit that," I said, and then laughed. It was the dumb type of thing kids said to each other in teen movies. Micah would've appreciated that joke.

Reed didn't respond and just looked glum.

"Just get her to tell you everything about this place, and we'll figure out a way out of here together, okay?"

"Sure," Reed said, but he sounded uncertain.

That night, Ames came to me while everyone else was sleeping. He was very quiet, not wanting to wake everyone else up. "Gareth has ordered I bring you to see him again. We have to be quiet. He asked that no one else find out about this."

I got up quickly and followed him out the door and through the corridors that led to Gareth's living area. It was dark and quiet, so it must've been after midnight.

We walked very quickly. Ames didn't say a word to me and I didn't say anything either. I was excited to talk to Gareth and tell him about what I saw in the training area and what Reed told me.

I walked in and Ames left immediately, with a

grim look on his face. I wondered what he thought about Gareth and me being together. I was just an innocent teenager to him. From the look on his face, I imagine it disgusted him.

"Hello, there," Gareth said, greeting me with a hug. He poured me a cup of hot tea and I curled up on the chair opposite where he sat down.

"Chelsea told Reed she's trying to get off the island," I said, cutting to the chase. I couldn't help but feel good about telling him about Chelsea's shadiness. I was the loyal one. The one that wouldn't turn on him no matter what.

"Are you sure?"

"That's what Reed told me. She volunteered this information herself and Reed is waiting to hear more."

"Hmmm . . . " Gareth looked troubled. "That doesn't sound like Chelsea."

"She's flirting with Reed, and I can tell something weird is going on with her and Odin too. I don't know what yet."

"What else have you found out?"

"Well, not much else yet, but I'm working on it."

I bit my lip, hoping the info about Chelsea would distract him enough not to ask about Elise. I feared he would be disappointed in me if he knew I'd deliberately not followed through with what he'd asked.

"So, what are you going to do about Chelsea?" I asked, wanting to hear about how she'd be punished.

"I'm not sure. I need to think about that and I want to dig a bit more—make sure Reed's not just exaggerating or misinterpreting things."

"He's not," I insisted.

"You're doing a good job, my dear. And that fight against Rose—you were very believable."

"Thank you, Gareth."

"But since I know you so intimately, I could tell you were holding back," he continued, leaning in toward me with eyebrows arched.

"Yes," I said, laughing. "She put up a fight, but not much."

"I'm learning you're quite the little actress," Gareth said, and I couldn't tell if he meant that as a compliment. "Aren't you?"

He gazed at me with an accusing glare.

"I'm here to do your bidding, Gareth, and nothing more."

He smiled and patted my leg. "Good. Now it's time you get back before anyone wakes up and finds out you're missing."

CHAPTER 15

I waited for Micah to show up in the training area for weeks and he never arrived. I really wanted the chance to talk to Gareth about it but Ames didn't take me to him again and I had no way of communicating with him without arising suspicions.

Where could Micah be? I wondered. *Had he been put up to battle in the Coliseum and been injured?* I sat up at night, unable to sleep, worrying about him. It was unlikely one of the other kids could've hurt him; Micah was a better fighter than anyone I'd ever seen. But he still could've been hit by a Suit's arrow or bullet if something happened that was out of his control—or if he was provoked in a way that he needed to defend himself.

All I wanted was confirmation that he was okay.

Eventually, we were ordered to the Coliseum for another round of fighting and I was feeling more and more despondent. All of us kids were painted for battle one by one, which felt humiliating to me. *Why was Gareth putting me through this without Micah? Was this another test?*

I didn't want to fight again—not that day. I was in no mood to fake it and act a part. I wanted to scream up to Gareth and yell to take me to Micah right away, wherever he was being held.

After we got ready, we learned that one of our training mates named Mato was put up against a new fighter, but Ames wouldn't—or couldn't—tell us who he was battling.

We were brought to the viewing deck that looked down on the Coliseum floor. I had no idea what was going to happen next. As we waited there, watching the people in the stands mill about,

talking with each other, holding court with their lovers, I felt impatient and annoyed. I was anxious for whatever was about to happen to just begin already.

Once the proceedings started and the gate raised, Micah walked in and Reed yelled out, trying to get his attention. I screamed down too, even though I could tell the crowd's cheers and the music blaring on the speakers would drown us out.

I knew Mato would be an easy opponent for Micah, and I was thrilled to see him in person again. He was okay. But where had he been? He didn't look injured or in distress, although he gazed around quickly to take in his surroundings. I thought I saw him smirk—just a little bit—as he was ushered to the center area, where Mato was waiting for him, looking nervous.

I was so confident in Micah's abilities that I was more eager to see him fight than anxious. I also hoped this meant we'd be reunited in the training arena afterwards.

As I anticipated, he took out Mato easily. I glanced down at Gareth who looked pleased by Micah's performance. It had been quick, but Micah was so impressive in his abilities that the people in the crowd cheered him heartily. They gave him a standing ovation.

As he left the arena, Micah looked up at us, catching my eye and calling out to me and to Reed.

I knew I'd be seeing Micah later and I couldn't wait to fill him in on everything Gareth had told me and to hear about what he'd been doing since we had arrived at the island.

Reed was called to fight next and he protested it, trying to pull away as he was taken down to the Coliseum floor. I was curious to see who he'd be fighting against, and was surprised when I saw a very tall, hooded man pulled out to the Coliseum against his will.

The way he walked—heavy on his feet, his long, gangly limbs and tan skin—I knew immediately who it was. True.

I was confused. I stood up to try to get a better look and scanned the crowd, searching for Titus. There he was, sitting behind Gareth. He was laughing and didn't look disturbed that True was being dragged out to fight.

What happened? I never liked True that much—he was usually an asshole to me and Micah—but Titus always defended him like a brother and let him do whatever he wanted.

Why had Gareth put True in the ring? And up against Reed?

They fought and suddenly, as True was attacking Reed, he stopped mid-stride and stared up at the stands, suddenly transfixed.

He spotted Titus and screamed, "You lied to me! I'm going to kill you!" His face contorted in anger and turned bright red. In that moment, Reed struck out, snatching a zapper from a White Suit and incapacitating True before striking him dead with a club.

He was fast, efficient, and didn't seem to be

perturbed by what he had just done—by killing a man. He was changing—I could see it. That's what fighting did to you. It became easier every time.

Micah came to our training area after a few days. I rushed over to see him when he entered, unable to help myself, and he lifted me up into the air and swung me around. We couldn't kiss right there. Reed was standing next to us and everyone else was still around, but the hug was amazing and I couldn't wait to get him by himself so we could share everything.

We went into training that afternoon, and during our break, I hung back to ensure everyone else got their water first. Finally, when everybody had cleared, I walked over to the fountain. A minute later, Micah was right behind me. I swung around and smiled at him.

"I've been waiting for you. Where have you been?"

"It's a long story," Micah said, leaning down to take a sip of water, not wanting to draw attention to us talking.

"Did you know True was killed . . . and by Reed?" I asked, still reeling over this development. I glanced back at Reed, who was talking to Ames.

"I did know that," Micah said, looking tense. "Titus told me what he was up to and I was the one who told Gareth about what True was doing."

"Well, what was he doing?" I asked, looking at him.

"It's a long story, but he was not following Gareth's orders taking care of the Littles, and Titus caught him."

"What happened though?" I asked.

Ames suddenly called out to us. "Okay, guys, time to get started again. We don't have time for chit chat, I'm afraid. Still much work to get done around here. Come on over."

I stared up at Micah, frustrated that we couldn't talk freely, and he just shrugged. Knowing this wasn't the time or place to press to learn more, we jogged back to where Ames was standing. It would have to wait.

"Odin and Reed are both pests, distracting Chelsea from finding happiness on the island—" Gareth told me, as we sat in the courtyard inside his living space.

I nodded, curious to hear where this conversation was headed.

"I thought Odin would be gone long ago, but he's like a cockroach—a cockroach that's ruining my relationship with my daughter. She thinks she'll be happier out there—in the real world—when I know from experience that the real world is no place for a girl like her. She wouldn't last a week before begging to come back. And what would people think—a beautiful girl like her just showing up out of thin air? Odin is just like his father—a troublemaker—and I fear he's created a rift between me and Chelsea that can't be repaired."

"But why is he a fighter?" I asked.

"He tried to kill me after he thought I killed his father. I had to protect myself and Chelsea against him. So now I've decided it's time I put two of my problems against each other and see who comes out on top."

"What do you mean?"

"I'm going to put Odin and Reed up against each other in the battle, and no matter what happens, I'm left with one less issue to deal with."

"But won't that just upset and alienate Chelsea further?" I asked, truly trying to understand the plan so I could help him.

"Maybe. But, I'm protecting the poor girl from herself. She's always had a penchant for getting herself in trouble, unlike you—" He reached over and patted my knee and smiled. "You, my dear, have always been perfect to me. It's proof to me what good genes and a structured upbringing can do for someone."

I felt flattered by his positive attention. He always reminded me why I was special, and had a knack for doing it when I was feeling confused or frustrated. Sometimes it was like he could read my thoughts entirely.

I knew if we could just smooth out all of the problems—Elise's escape, Chelsea's desire for a different life, and the security system glitches, Gareth would reunite me and Micah and let us live freely on the Praeclarus side of the island. That was all I wanted. But before that could happen, we had to uncover everything once and for all.

Ames came a minute later and escorted me back to my cell. I glanced at his wristlet—four twenty-two a.m. Everyone was still asleep and no one stirred when I slipped into my cell.

After some begging on my end, Gareth had graciously moved Micah's cell right next to mine, and

I hoped he would stir so he could come sit next to me on the other side of the bars and we could whisper about everything that was happening, and the plan.

But right now, he was sleeping. The moonlight streamed through the window that was cut into the wall, and I could see him clearly. I felt so lucky that he loved me and I loved him, and that Gareth supported us being together, especially when I heard him talk about Chelsea and that he didn't approve of her relationship with Odin.

I wondered if Chelsea was really planning something or if she was just frustrated and trying to figure out a way to get Gareth's attention. She'd be in for a rude awakening when Odin and Reed fought each other. I wasn't positive that Odin would win that fight. Reed was getting stronger and Odin struck me as overly confident in his abilities and the promise of leaving this place.

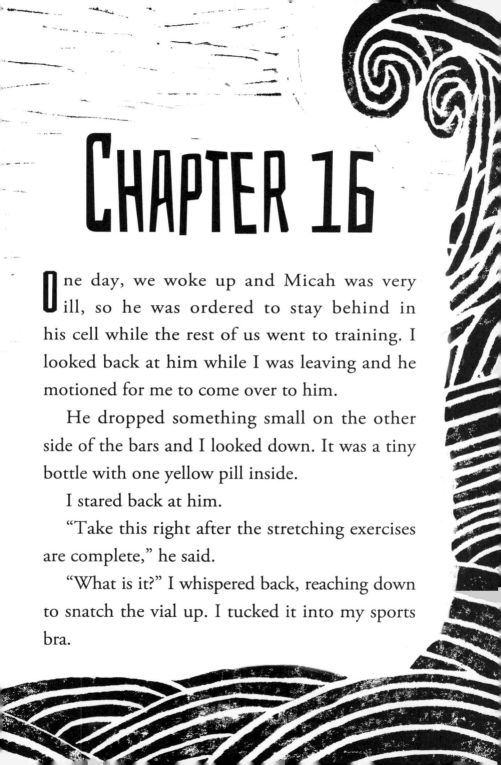

CHAPTER 16

O ne day, we woke up and Micah was very
ill, so he was ordered to stay behind in
his cell while the rest of us went to training. I
looked back at him while I was leaving and he
motioned for me to come over to him.

He dropped something small on the other
side of the bars and I looked down. It was a tiny
bottle with one yellow pill inside.

I stared back at him.

"Take this right after the stretching exercises
are complete," he said.

"What is it?" I whispered back, reaching down
to snatch the vial up. I tucked it into my sports
bra.

"A ticket to get some time together . . . now get going. They're waiting for you," Micah said, and motioned over to the main exit, where two Suits were looking impatient.

My heart beat fast in excitement. I didn't understand what the pill would do or where he got it, but I knew I could trust Micah and I wanted nothing more than to be with him.

Out in the training area, we went through our normal morning exercises with Ames. After we were done running through the many stretching exercises, I snuck over to the drinking fountain and quickly swallowed the pill, not thinking twice about it.

Within minutes, I started to feel really ill, like I was going to throw up and my stomach was clenching uncontrollably. I rarely got sick and I was miserable.

"Wow—Delphine?! Are you okay? You don't look so good," Reed said, running over to me and helping me to sit down.

My face felt flush and Ames came over.

"You look awful. Do you need to go to the infirmary?"

"No, I don't think so. I think I may just need to lay down and rest for a bit before coming back out to training. Is that alright?" I asked, looking up at Ames weakly.

"Yes, it seems like you need the rest," he said. "We need you back in fighting form soon, though. Gareth said he has special plans for you," he said, and then beckoned a Suit to come over.

The Suit led me to our living quarters and to my cell. My head was throbbing, my stomach was killing me, and I lay down on the cot immediately. I glanced over to Micah's cell and it looked like he was asleep. The Suit closed my cell and locked it, then went to return to the training area.

As soon as he left, Micah popped up out of bed and came over to the bars that separated us.

"How are you feeling?"

"Terrible. What the hell did you give me?"

"I know, but it only lasts about thirty minutes

and then you'll be back to normal. I've got a surprise for you," Micah said.

The door leading out clicked open and Titus
walked through, approaching us. He then came over
to my cell and opened it, allowing Micah to come
in.

"You guys have three hours—that's it—and
then I'll be back. Gareth is making sure no one else
is coming back here this morning, so you're both
safe. And we've switched the angle of the cameras—to give you a little privacy," he said, pointing
up at the video camera in the corner that was now
pointing to the neighboring cell.

I couldn't believe what I was hearing. I was anxious to feel back to normal so I could enjoy every
moment of being alone with Micah.

"It'll be about fifteen more minutes and you'll
feel better," Micah said, rubbing my back as he sat
next to me.

"What's going on?" I asked, looking up at him.

"Gareth is finally giving us some time together, just like he promised he would."

"Amazing," I said, reaching up to try to pull Micah in for a kiss, even though I was still feeling woozy.

"To talk," Micah said, pulling away, and looking at me sternly.

"Oh," I responded, unable to control my disappointment.

"At first—" He smiled, like he was teasing me.

"Okay, so what do we need to talk about?" I asked, looking up at him. My head was slowly starting to clear and I was feeling just a tiny bit better.

"The Praeclarus members have no idea that a revolt is being planned and we need to keep it that way."

"Revolt?"

"Gareth found out that Elise and maybe some of the other staffers are planning to try to band together to get off the island."

I thought about the security glitches that Gareth

had been so nervous about. This being part of Elise and maybe even Chelsea's plans as one big revolt was an unsettling notion. "What can we do?"

"Gareth wants to keep on putting Reed in battle to please Praeclarus. But I think he's the key to get more information about what is being planned—we have to help keep him alive," Micah explained.

I nodded my head and he continued.

"Praeclarus likes watching Reed fight. He's getting better and they like the novelty of knowing that it's Tim Mackenzie's son. But Gareth's conflicted."

"In what way?" I asked.

"He often prefers to do whatever Praeclarus demands of him. That's how he keeps everyone entertained, under his thumb, and loyal—so he feels like he must keep putting Reed in the Coliseum."

"Okay."

"But that means we have to move quicker to try to figure out what is going on. Gareth is going to loosen the lockdown after the Praeclarus members leave so Reed, Elise, and Ames can speak to each other more freely. Our job is to get Reed to talk to us—"

"By any means necessary?" I asked.

"Yes. Why, what do you have in mind?" Micah asked.

"Reed's always had a thing for me, right?"

"Yes, but he likes Chelsea right now."

"I'm not going to let that little obstacle stop me. I'm pretty sure I can get friendly with Reed and he'll open up and share everything. He always has loose lips."

"I trust you, although it won't be easy seeing you flirt with Reed, you know," Micah reached down and stroked my hair.

I was feeling better now and I looked around, just to confirm that we were truly alone and that no one else was coming.

"I've missed you, babe," and I put my arms

around his back and pulled him down on top of me.

"Me too . . . " Micah whispered, nuzzling his face into my neck. I reached and pulled his t-shirt off over his head.

He tugged at the bottom of my tank top and pulled it off easily.

"I've been waiting for this for too long," I murmured, as he took off my shorts and fumbled with his own pants.

We'd had sex many times before, and I knew Titus and Gareth realized it was happening. I was surprised they had never tried to stop us.

Feeling paranoid one day, I told Titus I had a question that I needed to ask him, but that I was embarrassed.

"So, I know you know about me and

Micah—and that we really, really like each other," I started, feeling my face turn red.

"Oh, that. Yes, I know what you're doing," he responded immediately, to my surprise. "And it's okay. It's a natural thing humans do when they like each other."

"I know," I said, just wanting to get this conversation over with as quickly as possible. "But my question is—do I need birth control?"

Titus looked up at me, surprised.

"I really don't want to get pregnant. I don't want a baby."

"Ahh, I see. I should've known this conversation would happen sooner or later." He put down his tablet and locked eyes with me.

"At this point, we don't think you need birth control. We believe that you are sterile. And so is Micah."

"Sterile? What does that mean?"

"It means that you can never have babies."

I let the words sink in for a moment, and

immediately felt relieved. But as we sat there, the words nagged at me.

"Is there something wrong with us?"

"No. You're created exactly the way Gareth envisioned. Don't you worry about that."

Back in our cell, when Micah and I were finished, we lay back on the bed and snuggled. He put his arms around me and we were quiet. We still had another hour together until a Suit would come back for us.

"What do you think about the Island?" I asked him.

"I think Gareth is capable of amazing things. It's hard to believe that one man created a whole new world just because he wanted to. I like it, though. I think it will make a good home for us once everything settles down. We'll get a little bunker just for us, sit on the beach together, go hunting, watch the fights, have babies—it will be a good life."

I didn't say anything about the babies, as I never shared with him my conversation with Titus. I had a feeling it would upset him and I didn't want to break this positive, happy façade that he was able to maintain all the time.

"What do you think is going to happen to the Littles?" I asked, thinking about the younger versions of me and Micah that still inhabited the Triangle. "Especially now that True is gone. What was that about, anyway? Can you tell me now why he was put in the Coliseum?"

"Okay—I'm sorry. It wasn't the right time when you asked me before. True was trying to contact the outside world to sell info about us and the Littles to the highest bidders. Titus caught him—and so we had to take care of it. The weird thing is that True claimed that Titus was in on it too—but we know that can't be true. Titus would never betray Gareth."

"What? True did that?"

I felt sick to my stomach, thinking that this person I'd known my whole life was trying to sell the Island's secrets. I knew True was an asshole, but this news still stung. I also didn't believe Titus could be in on it, but it did make me wonder if anyone was really who they seemed.

CHAPTER 17

We were getting ready in the morning for training when a Suit brought Reed in. He'd been in the hospital recovering from his Komodo tiger injuries for the past week and wasn't totally healed, but was doing a lot better. They'd given him some sort of anti-venom to help counteract the poison in the wound, and he was injured, but able to move and breathe freely—so he was lucky.

Gareth had told us that he was going to let him back into the main population early and let up on the mandatory lockdown to give everyone a chance to talk.

Micah and I were sure Reed would share

what he knew with us. He'd already implied that Ames, Elise, and even Chelsea were trying to figure out ways off the Island, and that they were on the brink of enacting their plan.

"Reed! Oh my goodness! I'm so happy you're okay!" I said as soon as he walked in, and Micah and I ran over and I hugged him. He winced and I pulled back.

"Oh, I'm so sorry. How are you feeling?" I asked, looking at him, concerned.

"I've been better," he said. "The question is, are you okay? I can't believe you came down to help me . . . what happened? The last thing I remember was you killing that animal, that thing, and then everything went dark. Why did you do that?"

"You needed help, Reed. I didn't think about it. I just did what was right in the moment."

"Where'd you learn to fight like that?" he asked, looking at me, amazed.

"Here, silly, what do you think we've been doing all this time?"

"And what about you, how are you, man?" Reed asked, turning to Micah.

"I'm okay." Micah looked around to see if anyone was listening, and then got quiet. "Have you heard any more about Elise and Ames's plan to get out of here?"

"No, I need to talk to them. Everything went to shit so they had to delay their plan. I have to get access to talk to them alone . . . but I'm not sure how. And I also need to talk to Chelsea. Have you guys seen her?"

Micah and I exchanged glances as if we were nervous to tell him the truth.

"Chelsea's in solitary confinement. Gareth put her there after what happened," I explained.

"What do you mean? What happened?" he asked, looking sick to his stomach.

"Chelsea jumped down from the stands against Gareth's will after I killed the creature," I explained.

"What? Why? I don't understand?"

"Because she wants off the Island, and she is fed up with everything she's witnessed. She told me she wants out of here."

"But, why is she in confinement?"

I shrugged. "Gareth is tired of her defying him. And to do it so publicly, in front of his friends and Praeclarus—it was really the last straw, I guess."

"Where is she?"

"We have no idea. Only people who really understand the Island would even be able to guess at that. Maybe Elise or Ames know?"

"We have to figure it out, okay? I can't let her rot away in some jail cell by herself while we all try to escape."

"Reed—you also can't stay here forever just to save Chelsea," Micah chimed in. "We may not have time."

"Yeah, Gareth is hell-bent on killing you. I'm sure I can't save you again," I said. "And I'll probably be put in the Coliseum next for defying Gareth.

He was really angry with me and swore I'd be up next. We must move quickly."

"Okay, okay," Reed said. "Well, we at least have to try to find her . . . it's the right thing to do."

"Yeah, it's true," I said, even though I thought it was idiotic that he cared so much for a girl that tried to get him killed.

"So, how are you going to get to see Elise?" I asked, changing the subject. And then I had an idea. "How about in the next training session, we both get injured and have to be sent to the infirmary at the same time?"

"But it will probably be Darby who cares for us, not Elise . . . " Reed said.

"Oh . . . " I had to think quickly and make up an excuse. "You didn't hear about that either?" I asked, glancing over at Micah, who looked at me, surprised, but I could tell he was ready to follow along.

"Darby got sick at the last match. He was

helping someone in the stands who had hurt himself, and he collapsed—right in front of everyone."

"Whoa, really?"

"Yeah, and he's in some sort of place where he has to rest for a while."

"How do you know all this?" Reed asked, looking at me confused.

"I overheard some Suits talking about it after we saw Darby collapse."

This was all a lie and I'd have to talk everything through with Gareth. It was the best I could do in the moment. Gareth would have to make sure Darby was out of the picture and that it was Elise who took care of us in the infirmary. I'd need to see Gareth right away to tell him.

"Reed, let's do this tomorrow. We don't have time to waste."

"How are we going to both get injured, though?" he asked, looking doubtful.

"Acting. Let's make sure we spar each other tomorrow, and it will get too heated. You will pretend you've torn something or re-injured yourself, and I will pretend that I have trouble breathing. Ames will want to believe it because he's on our side. He'll want you to get the opportunity to speak to Elise."

"Why wait until tomorrow?"

"You need at least one more day to recuperate. Tomorrow just pretend you're showboating and it gets out of hand."

At training later, I pulled Ames aside.

"I'm scared for my life, Ames. You have to help me."

"What do you mean?"

"I know Gareth wants me dead after that little display I pulled at the last fight." I tried to look scared and helpless as I said this.

"Yes, he's told me that you're next, as soon as the Praeclarus fights resume," Ames said, falling into my plan perfectly.

"Please! You need to help me! I can't die here! I just want off this island."

Ames looked concerned but didn't say anything

at first. Finally he grumbled, "How can I help you?"

"You need to bring me to Gareth again tonight, please. Please help me."

"He doesn't want to see you," Ames said, which I doubted was the truth, but was more his way to try to protect me.

"You don't understand. I need to try to talk some sense into him, and convince him not to kill me. I'll grovel. I'll beg. I'll do anything he wants me to do. Anything," I said, hamming it up, and trying to sound as scared as I could muster.

"I don't think this is a good idea," Ames said.

"I've run out of other options, Ames. You have to help me."

He was quiet for a moment, then said, "Okay, okay. I'll take you there but I don't think it's going to help. Gareth has a reputation of using girls and women, and then disposing of them. I don't think there's anything you can say to change his mind."

"It's my life. You have to let me try," I begged.

"Fine. Now get back to work. I'll come get you after everyone's asleep."

"Thank you," I said and I wanted to hug him. Not because I was actually thankful, but because I was so thrilled he fell for my ruse. I had to speak to Gareth before tomorrow no matter what.

That night before bed, I whispered through my cell bars to Micah, "We're good."

"Good luck," he whispered back, flashing me a smile.

I stayed up watching the silhouette of his body under his covers as he fell asleep, and I listened to the sounds of the other fighters breathing until Ames finally came to get me.

"You know I don't approve, but I wish you the best in changing his mind," he said, as we walked down the quiet hallways. I thought it was funny he kept on taking me to Gareth with no idea that we weren't lovers at all, and that we spent our evenings together plotting.

I was becoming an extension of Gareth's power, a way to expand his eyes and ears beyond the cameras and mics everywhere.

Ames led me in and quickly departed, leaving me to talk through the plan with Gareth. When I told him, Gareth was delighted that we'd set action in motion.

He trusted Darby, but to be safe, he'd visit him in his room in the morning and poison his coffee when Darby didn't expect it. Darby would quickly fall mysteriously ill, and would have to stay in his room all day.

Gareth would then reluctantly call on Elise to help both me and Reed when we became injured. When we were with Elise, Gareth would check on the infirmary surveillance to see if it went down while we were talking. That would confirm that there were other people helping Elise and Ames and that there was a coordinated effort to hide information from him as they plotted.

I'd play the innocent, asking questions about the plan and trying to get them to share as much as possible about what had already been plotted and what was in the works. I'd dig to see if Chelsea was actually involved or if she was a hanger-on, trying to latch herself on to the plan, to find any way to escape the Island.

I'd also figure out how many people were involved and who they were so we could determine the best course of response, and how much time we had to figure everything out.

We needed to stop everything before Reed contacted his dad. It would be catastrophic if Reed was able to reach his father and share what was happening on the Island—that Gareth was still alive, and anything about the Praeclarus members.

I was as sure as Gareth that Tim Mackenzie would use everything he had to expose the Island and Praeclarus—each member an extremely powerful and influential person harboring this dark secret. It was information that would cause turmoil across the world and would certainly put an end to the Island as we knew it.

If Gareth lived through the siege, he'd be jailed for life at the very least, and I had no idea what would happen to me and Micah when the Littles were discovered. We would probably be put in a lab and studied every day, poked and prodded and tested to death.

I knew helping Gareth was a life-or-death situation for us, and I was determined to do whatever I could to save myself and prove to Gareth that I deserved to live freely outside the Triangle. Then, once he was gone, Micah and I could continue his legacy and ensure that this place was protected forever.

Ames came back to get me just before dawn.

"I think my plan worked and that Gareth is going to give me a reprieve next battle."

He raised his eyebrows and looked doubtful—like he felt sorry for me.

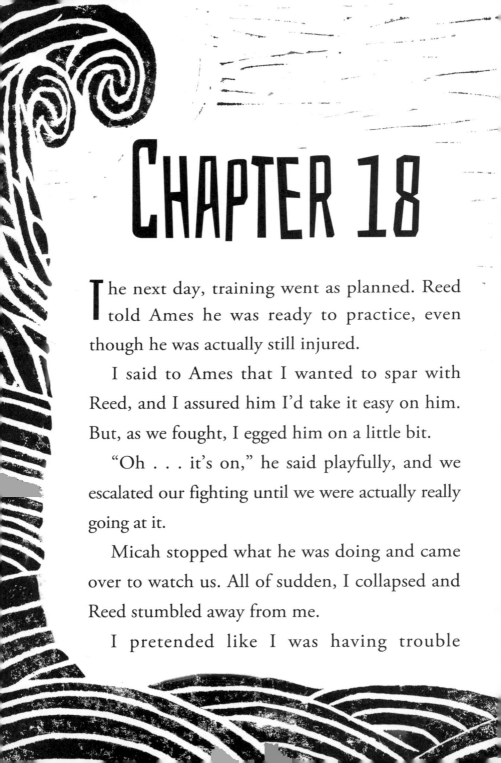

CHAPTER 18

The next day, training went as planned. Reed told Ames he was ready to practice, even though he was actually still injured.

I said to Ames that I wanted to spar with Reed, and I assured him I'd take it easy on him. But, as we fought, I egged him on a little bit.

"Oh . . . it's on," he said playfully, and we escalated our fighting until we were actually really going at it.

Micah stopped what he was doing and came over to watch us. All of sudden, I collapsed and Reed stumbled away from me.

I pretended like I was having trouble

breathing and Reed pointed to his shirt, which was dripping in blood.

I'd re-opened one of his wounds.

Ames ran over to us. "Shit guys, I told you to take it easy. What were you thinking?"

"Sorry," Reed said. "But help Delphine . . . look at her . . . "

He pointed to me and I continued to act like I was really struggling.

"I . . . can't . . . breathe . . . " I gasped and Ames looked puzzled and disturbed.

"Geez. This isn't like you at all. I guess you guys have to go to the infirmary. One sec . . . "

He stopped and spoke something into his wristlet and moments later, two Suits came through the big gates to take us away.

Micah called out after us, "Take care of them, okay?"

I scanned the faces of the other fighters as the Suits helped me out of the training area. No one

else seemed concerned. It was almost like they were annoyed.

I was relieved to see Elise there in the infirmary waiting for us, not Darby. Gareth had taken care of his part of the plan. *Of course.*

Elise looked us over.

"What's happened here?" She ushered both of us to the examination table before turning to the Suits, who were standing there waiting for direction. "You two may leave."

They shuffled out the door and closed it behind them. As soon as they did, Reed started talking.

"Are we okay?" he asked, glancing up at the camera.

Elise looked at her wristlet for confirmation. "Yes, we can talk freely."

I tried not to look disturbed or surprised by this,

but I was shocked at how quickly someone could respond to turn off the surveillance.

"Before we talk though everything, Reed, I need to take care of you," she said, coming over to remove his shirt. He was a good-looking guy and I couldn't help but smile shyly at him, like I enjoyed what I saw.

The gash on his shoulder had reopened and was bleeding a lot. While Elise cleaned it up and dabbed a numbing cream on it, she glanced over at me.

"You seem to be feeling better . . . " she said, and I couldn't read if there was a hint of accusation in her tone or if she was just observing.

"Yes, much better, but I am thankful to rest. I think I was just being worked too hard out there," I replied.

"Hmmm . . . " Elise said as she sewed up Reed's shoulder. "Well, I'm glad you're feeling good now. It's not like you to get so winded, is it?"

"No, not at all. I used to have asthma as a

kid, though," I said, feeling self-conscious at her questions.

"We can talk openly in front of her, don't worry," Reed said, as if sensing Elise's doubts. "She's one of us."

I wanted to laugh, since that was the farthest statement from the truth in so many ways.

"So, what's happening with the plan?" Reed asked, looking anxious. "We need to get out of here soon, before one of us gets killed. Delphine is in serious danger . . ."

"We all are," Elise said. "Thankfully, I think we can move forward with the next phase of the plan in the next couple of days. We need to do it before the following round of Praeclarus members arrive in a week."

"Why? Don't we want to take them out?" I asked.

"Oh yes, but we'll do that from the safety of the real world. We know intimate details about all of them and we can expose them when we get to safety. We'll make sure everyone pays, don't you worry about that."

"So, what is happening? How am I contacting my dad?" Reed asked.

"Ames and our cohorts have re-programmed all of the Island computers. Gareth knows that something fishy is going on with the surveillance systems—he keeps on hounding the security team to figure it out, but conveniently—they haven't been able to get to the root of the problem."

"That's amazing," I said, trying to sound excited and not pissed off.

"But Gareth doesn't even know the half of it. We're in control of everything now. He's too far removed from the intricacies of the computer system and he doesn't know who he can trust to give him truthful information any longer. But the reality is, we've re-mastered it all."

"What does that mean?" Reed asked.

"Everything just looks like it is running smoothly, but we're in control now. We can open all the gates, we control all surveillance, and we can communicate to the outside world."

"So why don't you just contact the news or government embassies and get them to help us?" Reed asked.

Elise laughed at this, like Reed had told a funny joke.

"Do you know who is in Praeclarus?" she asked us.

"Celebrities? Rich people?" I guessed.

"And world leaders—some of the most powerful men in the world."

"And . . . ?" Reed asked, not understanding.

"And if they find out that someone from the Island is reaching out asking for help, they'll order Gareth to use his Kill Switch."

"What's the Kill Switch?" I asked, as this was news to me too.

"Gareth has this whole island rigged with explosives and can blast everything out of the water with one short code inputted into his wristlet. Only he has the code, but we know it can be done."

"How do you know this?" I asked.

"Because I helped build the Island too. I've been here from the beginning and I know all of its intricacies."

"So, why do you want to reach Reed's dad?"

"We'll blackmail him with Reed's life to stay quiet, but to help us," Elise explained. "But, as soon as we leave, we'll expose everything, don't you worry. And we'll do it before Gareth even has the chance to think about using the switch."

"But why doesn't he just do it now, when things are starting to come apart?" Reed asked.

"Gareth is an extremely prideful man. He's spent decades making this island into his version of a perfect world—a world where moral boundaries do not need to be obeyed. He won't let go of the Island and what it means to him without a fight."

"So what's the plan?" Reed asked, and I could tell he was feeling impatient.

"The first step is to get in contact with your dad. We need to do it when no one is tracking your every movement—"

"When?" I asked.

"It will have to be the middle of the night, as everyone else is sleeping."

"Okay, when can we do that?" I pressed and Elise raised her eyebrows at me slightly.

"I think Ames is ready for tomorrow night."

"How is it going to work?" Reed asked.

"Ames or I will come get you in the middle of the night, but you have to be very quiet and not wake up anyone else."

"And what about the Suits? What if they see you guys?" I asked, digging a little more.

"We've ensured that the Suits that will be patrolling the training area and security bank are friendly."

"And what about Gareth?" Reed asked. "How can we make sure he won't be alerted to this? If

Gareth discovers us, we'll definitely be dead. No doubt about it."

"Well, we're still figuring that part out now—that's another reason why we need another day . . ."

"And what happens after we contact my dad?" Reed looked concerned.

"Well, he's going to have to determine where we are, and quickly send help—"

"How did you figure all of this out?" I asked. I couldn't believe they managed to work around Gareth's complex security.

"Bertram was working on this before he was killed—"

"Wait—who is Bertram?" Reed asked.

"Odin's dad—and the creator of many of the Island's security systems."

Before Reed could interject more, Elise kept talking rapidly. "Anyway, he left us very secretive instructions. We had to piecemeal clues he'd scattered across the island. It took a very long time to find all of the clues and to put them together. Bertram was obviously very scared for his life—and likely for the life of his son, Odin—and he took extreme precaution to ensure that the information wouldn't be discovered easily."

"He sounds like a very smart guy," I said.

"Yes, he was the best, and I loved him very much," Elise said wistfully. "And then, when the time comes and Reed's dad finally finds us, we will open all the gates, and let everyone out of their cages, even the Creatures. We'll escape and we'll leave the Creatures, Gareth, and the Suits that are loyal to Gareth behind."

"I love this plan," Reed said.

"And Gareth will have to decide then whether or not to use his Kill Switch—" she continued, "when his back is up against the wall and he's about to be exposed and imprisoned, and all of his friends will be exposed as well. It will be interesting to see what he does—kill everything and not face the music, or let his Island be discovered? I think he's so obsessed with what he did here that he'd rather rot in jail than burn this place to the ground."

Elise didn't know that I was one of the clones. She'd be in for a rude awakening when a bunch of younger versions of me and Micah walked out. I realized that maybe we could let them go early— the cast of soldiers—and have them do Gareth's dirty business without ruining the whole island. There were more of us being raised in the nursery now, so all was not lost.

"This plan sounds like it just might work," Reed said, looking optimistic. "How long will it take for my dad to get here?"

"Probably a few days to figure out where we are. We'll have to play it cool while we wait, but I'm hoping he can figure it out before the next round of Praeclarus members are set to arrive—and it will take several days after that for any crews to reach us. It will be much messier and more difficult if we have to deal with the Praeclarus members as well, but that might be the reality."

Reed nodded.

"So, how many Suits are on our side?" I asked, and I saw Elise look me over with a strange gaze, like she was turning over something in her mind again and again.

"There are about fifty of us who are ready to take a stand."

"Whoa," I couldn't help but say out loud. "That is good."

I guessed there were nearly two hundred staffers in total, so this number was actually quite significant. How had they planned this all, and what were we going to do to make sure we took them all out?

CHAPTER 19

Later that day, Ames came up to me. "Gareth wants to see you tonight—over dinner—you must've said or done something right," he said, looking me over, and then as if disturbed by his own thought, shook his head and sighed, not even hiding his disgust.

"Well, I'll do whatever I have to do to not be killed—don't judge," I said, trying to sound like I cared and that I was scared, but I couldn't wait to talk to Gareth and tell him the extent of the problem.

I wasn't sure how he was going to handle it or what he was going to do. Fifty people revolting out of two hundred was a significant portion, and those people wouldn't be easily replaceable. They were necessary to keep the Island running smoothly—to make our meals, to tend to the gardens, to keep the prisoners in line. Everything would be thrown off balance if fighting actually began, and Gareth would have to figure out how to contain it all without burning the whole Island to the ground.

I had so much to say to him, and we had much we needed to figure out right away. I updated Micah as quickly as I could by the water fountain before we were called back over, and he looked at me wide-eyed, like he was scared. I hadn't seen that expression very often and it annoyed me more than anything.

"It'll be okay," I said. "Gareth always has a plan for everything."

Ames came to get me later that night, right before dinner time. "You ready to go?"

"I guess," I said, not wanting to sound too eager, but like I dreaded that I was being summoned to Gareth.

As we walked through the hallways, I tried to memorize each turn and all of the steps I took and how we got from point A to point B. I looked for ways to escape, doors to duck into, and any way I could run and hide if I needed to when the time came.

Ames looked back at me. "You're awfully quiet tonight," he said.

"Just thinking about everything," I said, which was the truth. Gareth would need to come up with a plan to contain everything quickly, but he'd first have to figure out who he could trust. I knew he could count on me, Micah, Titus, and the scientists, but that was it, as far as I knew.

We went inside Gareth's room and he looked at

me and smiled widely, like he had no care in the world.

"You're a sight for sore eyes," he said, reaching out for me, and eyeing Ames to leave us alone. "Have dinner brought in now, and come back at midnight. I don't want her staying longer than I need her," he said to Ames. I rolled my eyes at Ames for effect and he looked like he felt genuinely bad for me.

Almost immediately, a Suit wheeled in a cart and promptly left again. Our dinner was laid out on two plates accompanied by one glass of red wine, and a glass of water for me. Gareth didn't allow me to drink, but after tasting the beer at the party, I didn't feel like I was missing all that much.

"I have so much to tell you—" I blurted out once we were alone, but Gareth waved me off.

"In a moment dear. I'm ravenous, and our food is warm—"

I knew he wouldn't be up for talking until after we'd dug into our food, so I dutifully began to eat the gourmet meal. It was a delicious cut of grilled fish and vegetables—and Gareth sipped his wine as he listened to me share everything about what was happening and what Elise, Ames, Reed, and others were planning.

His face was serious and he didn't react. He was silent and I wondered what sort of rage was boiling under the surface. I wasn't sure if even I wanted to see that.

As I was telling him, his face suddenly turned pale and he looked like he was beginning to sweat, like he was clammy. He started to shake and his body froze up just before he slid onto the floor.

"Get Elise!" he managed to yell.

"What?" I screamed out, feeling panicky. "Why Elise? I should get Darby, or . . . or . . . Titus . . . "

"Elise!" Gareth yelled out, and his body wasn't stopping as it twitched again and again. I felt terrified all of a sudden—what was happening to him?

I ran for the door, prepared to out myself completely to run to find Elise. I had no idea where she'd be right now, but as I flung the door open, I was shocked to see her standing there.

"Wait . . . what?" I stuttered, totally confused. What was she doing here?

She pushed past me, and walked over to Gareth, looking down at him.

"Well, well, well . . . look at this . . . " she said, peering at him with curiosity as his body shook.

"Help him!" I screamed, running over to lift him up off the ground, so his head would stop banging against the floor.

She turned a twisted smile at me. "Just what I thought—my little traitor. So, you're on his side, are you?"

"Oh . . . I . . . " I stammered, not sure what to say. "Please, can you help him?"

"Yes, I suppose, but I need you to tell me something first," she said, putting down her medical bag and kneeling down, peering into my eyes, completely ignoring Gareth as he trembled in my arms.

"What?" I screamed out, desperate. "What do you need to know?"

"Where are you from, love?"

"What do you mean?" I cried, not understanding.

"Where were you born?" she asked, looking at me with curiosity.

"I . . . I . . . " and suddenly the words were lost as I tried to come up with an answer and Gareth howled angrily beneath me.

"I thought so. I couldn't quite put my finger on it—you—earlier today. You seemed off. Like you were trying to be someone that you're not," she said, as she opened up her medical bag and pulled out a giant needle. I flinched, wondering if it was for me.

"And I thought about it and I thought about it, and your eyes—those beautiful green eyes, well, they're difficult to forget. And I'm surprised I did. And then I remembered you had that little tiny heart-shaped birthmark on your shoulder," she said, pointing to it. "So then, when I put two and two together, I knew who you were."

She lifted up Gareth's shirt as she talked, smiling just a little bit. Gareth had a huge scar down the length of his chest.

"I remember you as a little baby. My Zeta. You were the seventh version of the girl we tried to create, and you lasted longer than the others. But I was fed up with the experiments and wanted to leave the Island, yet Gareth wouldn't let me and banned me from the Hangar and all the experiments that were happening there."

I stood there, a mixture of impressed and scared that she caught on.

"He told me you died," she continued. "You and the baby boy. But look at you here—" she said, gazing at me up and down. "Where has he kept you all these years? And how many others of you are out there? And where is that baby boy now?" she asked.

I needed to protect Micah. "I have no idea."

Elise raised her eyebrows, as if she didn't believe me. "Interesting . . . " she murmured, as she plunged the giant needle into Gareth's heart and he sat bolt upright almost instantaneously.

"You bitch . . . " he shrieked, heaving, spit forming at the corners of his mouth.

"But, why did you save him?" I asked, confused.

"Remember the Kill Switch? Well, it is embedded in his heart. When it stops, this whole place goes—" she said. "We need to keep him alive—for now."

She eyed me thoughtfully. "But what are we going to do with you?"